ROMANCE IN A WINTER WONDERLAND

MARCIA LYNN McCLURE

Published by Distractions Ink
1290 Mirador Loop N.E.
Rio Rancho, NM 87144

Published by Distractions Ink
©Copyright 2017 by M. Meyers
A.K.A. Marcia Lynn McClure
Cover Photography by © Rodney Saul/Dreamstime.com
Cover Design and Interior Graphics by Sandy Ann Allred/Timeless Allure

First Printed Edition: December 2017
First Hardcover Edition: December 2017

McClure, Marcia Lynn, 1965—
Romance in a Winter Wonderland: a novel/by Marcia Lynn McClure.

ISBN: 978-0-9996274-2-6

Library of Congress Control Number: 2017918177

Printed in the United States of America
.

To My Sweet, Wonderful, Amazing Daughter, Sandy—
For cracking up so hard, and so many times,
over my 1977 Luke Skywalker journal entry!
You are sooooo much of my joy, Roni Pony! I love you!
~Mom

AND my sincerest thanks to anyone and everyone else
who enjoyed a good laugh over said journal entry!
My special thanks to the clever friend who created the hashtag,
#BoomBoomFoxy!

CHAPTER ONE

Keeley stared out the window of her parents' SUV as they traveled toward Snow Creek Ranch. The fresh snow and frost that had fallen the night before blanketed the ground like a soft, white, far-flung down comforter. The trees—with each and every visible limb and trunk thoroughly veiled in glistening hoarfrost—lent such a dreamy sense of bejeweled, diamond-gilded majesty to the enchanting winter wonderland that Keeley almost forgot she was not at all thrilled about spending the entire Christmas holidays with her dad's extended family—even if they were staying at the cabins at Snow Creek.

It wasn't that Keeley De Carlo didn't love her aunts, uncles, and cousins. She did! But she had just grown to relish finding a few unhurried, more serene days during the last few weeks of December. She enjoyed capturing quiet moments here and there, moments to linger in the calm tranquility of an evening—an evening spent sitting in a darkened room with miniature lights on a Christmas tree and the lovely flickering flames of candles as the only illumination, with soothing, instrumental Christmas music playing softly in the background. She figured that, even though each family had its own cabin, there wouldn't be much time for savoring the season with a mug of hot chocolate alone midst peace and quiet.

However, the Christmas season was Keeley's joy no matter what the circumstances were, and she was determined to enjoy every minute of it. For Keeley, Christmas wasn't just once a year—or even one month a year. For Keeley, Christmas simmered in her heart all year long—like a warm, sweet, comfortable mug of mulled cider. Every year, beginning about mid-March, Keeley's Christmas tinglings began.

For as long as Keeley could remember, she'd called her love for Christmas her "Christmas tinglings." As her mom had told her years before, Keeley had been about three years old when she'd first announced, "My Christmas tinglings are in me!" after playing in the sandbox one hot summer day. Of course, as Keeley had been only three years old, Keeley's father always said it was more accurate to say that she had announced, "My Chwistmas tingwings er in me!" But either way, everyone in Keeley's family understood that Keeley had been a Christmas girl from birth—or at the very least from the first moment she could express herself in a sentence.

All year long Keeley looked forward to Christmastime— daydreamed about wrapping gifts with pretty wrapping paper and glitter-embellished wire ribbon. All year long she sporadically hummed Christmas music to herself when working, shopping, cleaning, or making things to give as Christmas gifts. Most times she was entirely unaware she was humming them. But her grandmother had always told her that it was a sign of a happy heart.

So she didn't worry too much about it—even after someone had tapped her on the shoulder in a bookstore when she was a teenager and said, "Uh…you do realize you're humming Christmas carols out loud, right? And it's June?" Keeley's grandma had always been the wisest woman anyone, including Keeley, had ever known. She figured if the pinch-faced, middle-aged woman who pointed out her humming didn't have a happy enough heart to hum Christmas carols to herself in June, then it was just sad for the woman and not for Keeley.

All year long Keeley De Carlo gleaned inexplicable joy from thinking about happy things to do for others, making gifts, looking forward to decorating the Christmas tree, and doing all other things Christmassy. All year long she wondered why the Christian world wasn't always demonstratively joyous over the birth of Christ—in the birth of the Savior—more visibly thankful that He had chosen to sacrifice His life for the sake of each and every human being ever born. Yep—all year long Keeley loved Christmas. Until Christmas Day, that was. By noon on Christmas Day, Keeley found herself wanting to move beyond the Christmas of whatever year it had been and begin wandering with delight toward the next year's Christmas.

Of course, few people were aware of how deeply Keeley loved, looked forward to, and even needed Christmas. Her parents were aware of it, of course, as well as her two older brothers and their families and her little sister, Paisley. They all knew that a family reunion away from home was not Keeley's ideal for Christmas. Still, family reunions were an important tradition, and like her family, Keeley cherished tradition—even if they were stressful, inconvenient, and often not idealistic.

"You're not pouting, are you, Keys?" Paisley asked.

Keeley smiled, even giggled a little as she looked to her sister sitting in the seat to her right.

"I'm not pouting, Paiz," Keeley reassured her sister, "just marveling at how beautiful it is up here...so white and perfectly unmarred, you know?"

"Yeah!" Paisley sighed, smiling. "It's so pretty! I keep expecting to see little fairies skating along the tree branches or something."

"Oooo! That would be wondrous, wouldn't it?" Keeley exclaimed.

Paisley nodded, her eyes glistening with the beautiful naiveté of childhood.

Keeley studied her little sister a moment—marveled at how much she looked like Keeley had when she'd been six years old. Paisley had Keeley's brown eyes, Keeley's brown hair, and Keeley's thick, dark eyelashes. Both Paisley and Keeley had petal-pink lips and small noses—"button noses," her grandma had always called them. Born when Keeley was fourteen—"a quite unexpected but wonderful surprise," as Keeley's mother explained it—Paisley was growing up very differently than Keeley and her older brothers had. Technology was exploding—bursting bigger and bigger with each passing day— and Keeley sometimes felt sorry for Paisley for having to grow up in a world where two-year-olds could manipulate a cell phone better than they could a bucket of wooden blocks. Keeley wished Paisley could have more freedom, more time to be bored. Why, when Keeley had been Paisley's age, she hadn't even had to ride in a booster seat in the car, let alone a high-end, techy car seat. Nevertheless, as she studied Paisley sitting in a car seat that looked so comfortable one would've thought La-Z-Boy had produced it, Keeley simply determined to do what she'd always vowed to do since the day Paisley was born—make certain her baby sister found moments of tranquility and moments of boredom so that her young mind could ponder, create, and imagine.

Therefore, exhaling a sigh of resolve, Keeley offered, "You'll love tubing up here, Paiz! The snow is so soft that when you fly off your tube, it feels like you're landing in a big, fluffy puff of cotton candy!"

Paisley's brown eyes widened. "Oh, I love cotton candy!" she exclaimed.

"I know!" Keeley giggled. "And even though snow doesn't *taste* like cotton candy, it's so nice and cold and *so* yummy! We'll remind Mom to put some cream and vanilla in some cups of snow for us to eat, okay? It's different than cotton candy, but it's still scrumptious!"

"Mmm! It's making me hungry, Keys!" Paisley giggled.

"Me too," Keeley agreed.

"We're almost there, girls," Joe De Carlo told his daughters from his seat behind the steering wheel. "I for one am ready for a long stretch. I feel like I've been driving for days."

"That's because you *have* been driving for days," Cynthia De Carlo said, reaching over from her place in the front passenger's seat to massage the back of her husband's neck.

"Idaho in December," Joe sighed. "What were my sisters thinking when they planned this?"

Cynthia smiled, answering, "As they were planning it in June, I'm sure they were thinking a wintery Christmas family reunion would be magical."

"Magical, huh?" Joe scoffed. "What will be magical is if we all manage to arrive safely and don't die of cabin fever."

"What's cabin fever, Daddy?" Paisley asked, her eyes wide with trepidation. "I don't want to get sick! And I certainly don't want to die!"

"Cabin fever is just a term people used to say that they're getting tired of being in the house all the time," Cynthia explained. "You won't get sick, baby. None of us will."

Keeley giggled when her father mumbled, "Speak for yourself," under his breath.

"And look, Paiz!" Keeley's mom exclaimed then. "We're here already!"

"We are?" Paisley squealed with excitement

"We sure are," Cynthia confirmed. "And look how gorgeous it is! Oh, I've always loved Snow Creek…but especially in wintertime. Why don't we come more often, Joe? It's just beautiful!"

Even Keeley's rather moody expectation that the family reunion would ensure that Christmas would be difficult to enjoy that year dissipated as she caught sight of Snow Creek Ranch up ahead. Even in the daytime, the white lights were on, strung on every eave and window frame of the large, two-story lodge near the entrance to the ranch, beckoning travelers to nestle into its warm, cozy, fire-lit interior.

"Dad," Keeley began, "were you able to get the Cozy Cabin reserved for us?"

"Are you kidding, Keys?" Joe exclaimed. "The minute your aunt Krystal told me we were gonna have the reunion at Snow Creek, I hung up the phone and called. I wanted to make certain *we* got the Cozy Cabin."

"My hero!" Keeley giggled.

"Is the Cozy Cabin the best or something?" Paisley inquired.

Keeley smiled as she looked at her little sister to see the adorable expression of puzzlement she often wore puckering her brow.

"Well, I think so," Keeley answered.

"Why?" Paisley asked.

Used to answering hundreds of her little sister's questions every day, Keeley said, "Well, for one thing, it has a covered front porch, with big, comfortable chairs to sit on so that we can drink hot chocolate and watch the snow and frost fall under the moonlight without getting too cold and wet. But I like the bedrooms and front room the most. You remember, don't you? We came a couple of summers ago, and I remember you loved our bedroom because there wasn't a flat ceiling. You could just look up into the triangle of the roof overhead."

"Oh! I do kind of remember!" Paisley interrupted. "There were big tree things above us!"

"Yes! The big, long logs—the beams that support the roof. That's right!" Keeley encouraged.

"Is that the place where there were fireplaces in every room made out of rocks?" Paisley asked.

"Yep, that's the place," Keeley affirmed, delighted that Paisley could remember a place she'd last been to when she was only four years old.

"Oh! Oh! And there was a bathtub in the bathroom…a bathtub with golden feet! I remember being afraid it would just walk away, and I'd never get to take a bath in it. Ha ha ha!"

"That's right," Cynthia giggled. "I had forgotten about that! We had to let you take a bath every morning *and* every night because you were so worried you wouldn't get to play in it as much as possible."

Joe chuckled. "And you kept asking if we could get some bears to come in and snuggle with us."

Everyone laughed—even Paisley.

"Well, I was just a kid then, Daddy," she offered.

"Oh, that's right," Joe said, winking at Keeley by way of the rearview mirror. "I had forgotten."

"And we put marshmallows on sticks and stuck them in the fire and then ate them," Paisley continued.

It was obvious Paisley's memory was being jogged. In truth, it was more like her memory was sprinting.

"And there were soft, warm quilts on the bed—red and brown ones—and big, squishy pillows too," she prattled.

"Oh, we've opened a can of worms now," Cynthia mumbled to Joe.

"And the sinks were all like big bowls sitting on top of the counters…not like our sinks at home where you reach down into them. Remember, Mommy? I had to use a stool, or you guys had to lift me up to wash my hands," Paisley continued. "Oh, and the fires smelled so good—like Christmas trees—and there were wooden toys in a wooden box in the family room and lots of old books on the bookshelves and pretty rugs everywhere. I remember playing on one and pretending I was riding a polar bear! Oh, I'm so excited now! This is a place I act'lly remember!"

"Well, I'm glad, sweetie," Cynthia chirped. "See? I told you it would be fun to come here for Christmas!"

Again Paisley's brows puckered as she looked to Keeley. Trying her best to whisper, she asked, "And Mom and Dad remembered to tell Santa we were going to be here for Christmas and not at home, right?"

"Right," Keeley assured her. And although she forced a smile of encouragement for her little sister's sake, Keeley felt a sadness pinch her heart in knowing that this may well be the last year Paisley could bathe in the wondrous bliss of believing—of wholeheartedly, undoubtfully knowing that Santa Claus still lived—that St. Nicholas hadn't died in 343 AD.

Still, inhaling with a determination to keep from knowing heartache for Paisley's sake, Keeley giggled and whispered, "What did you ask Santa for anyway? You never have told me."

Paisley smiled, moving her eyebrows up and down—her familiar indication that she had something impish on her mind—and answered, "I asked him to bring me a Jack Sparrow calendar and to bring you a boyfriend! See? I took care of us both this year...completely on my own!"

Keeley laughed. "You asked Santa to bring you a Jack Sparrow calendar? I thought you asked Mom and Dad for that?"

Paisley shrugged. "I did," she admitted. "But you know Mom." Again Paisley attempted to whisper, saying, "She thinks I'm too young for Jack Sparrow...even though I told her I know he's not a real person I could marry someday."

Keeley smiled, winked at Paisley, and said, "Well, it was good thinking, asking Santa for it. He'll come through, I know he will." Of course, Keeley exchanged glances with her mother—silently communicating that the Jack Sparrow calendar Keeley had purchased and wrapped as her Christmas gift for Keeley would need to be swapped out with one of the ones Santa was planning on giving to her.

"And he'll come through for you too, Keys," Paisley said. "It's about time you had a boyfriend and got married, you know."

Even though a boyfriend and marriage were sore spots for Keeley, she nodded and smiled anyway. After all, it wasn't Paisley's fault Keeley was so super picky about guys—so set on waiting for just the right man she knew could make her happy and that she could make happy in return.

"Here we are!" Cynthia exclaimed as Joe pulled the SUV into a parking place in front of the Snow Creek Ranch main office.

"Hallelujah," Joe sighed. He put the vehicle in park, turned the engine off, and turned in his seat to look at Paisley and Keeley. "You girls ready for a wild and wonderful Christmas with the De Carlo crazies?"

Keeley knew her dad was stressed about the family reunion. It was why she admired him all the more for pasting on a smile and feigning excitement—for everyone else's sake.

"Yay! De Carlo crazies! Yay!" Paisley cheered.

"Yay!" Keeley joined, winking at her dad.

"Let's get checked in so we can go to the cabin and rest before the first 'event' tonight," he said, making quotation marks with his fingers at the word *event*.

"Yeah! Let's get checked in, Daddy!" Paisley agreed. "But do I have to rest? I'm not tired at all."

"That's because you're young and innocent," Joe said, still smiling. "Now come on, let's go in. I bet they have free cocoa and candy canes at the front desk."

Paisley had unbuckled her car seat harness and shot out of her seat before Keeley had even taken another breath.

"Free hot chocolate?" Paisley squealed. "This place should be bombed!"

"This place is *the* bomb, you mean, sweetie," Cynthia corrected through her giggle.

As Keeley unbuckled her seat belt, she looked up to see a man step out of the cabin that was the Snow Creek Ranch office and start toward them.

"Thank you, Santa Claus," she mumbled to herself—for the man walking toward them was unquestionably the most attractive, the most well-formed, the most striking, the most handsome, sexiest man she had ever seen!

He looked to be in his mid-twenties. He wore jeans, weathered comp-toe work boots, and a classic barn coat that hung open to reveal the black-and-red flannel shirt beneath it. But it wasn't his manly, capable attire that so captivated Keeley—left her mouth agape and her eyes widened. It was his clean-cut dark brown hair, downright seductive oval, almost rectangular eyes, square jaw, and sensational movie-star smile!

"Boom-boom-foxy!" Paisley said as she leaned over Keeley to stare at the man who had reached their SUV and was offering a friendly handshake to her father.

"Way, way, way boom-boom-foxy," Keeley breathed as she watched the man greet her father. She was even too distracted by male physical perfection to giggle over Paisley's use of their secret term of describing a cute boy or handsome man—*boom-boom-foxy*, which had originated when she and Paisley had been reading through some of Keeley's old diaries from sixth grade. Like her little sister, Keeley had also secreted la passion for Johnny Depp as Jack Sparrow. Her movie star crush began when she was six years old as well, with Disney's first Pirates of the Caribbean movie, continued through the second adventure, and when the third movie was released, Keeley had written in her diary about it.

Went to see the best adventure movie ever with Mom and Dad today…the third Pirates of the Caribbean one! Johnny Depp played Jack Sparrow again! Boom-Boom-Foxy! Keeley had written. After reading the diary excerpt aloud to Paisley—and then explaining that boom-boom-foxy! meant Jack Sparrow was handsome and she loved him for it—Paisley had burst into laughter and repeated the phrase over and over and over. Oh, it was an archaic term, to say the least—contrived of different words she'd heard her aunts use over the years when referring to old actors from the 1970s and '80s. Still, Paisley's wonderful sense of humor and tendency to think more maturely than other kids her age had enabled her to find amusement in her older sister's secret middle school diary lingo. Therefore, Keeley and

Paisley had adopted boom-boom-foxy as their shared phrase to denote good-lookingness.

"Maybe I should hurry and write to Santa again, tell him this guy is here, and—" Paisley began.

"And these are my daughters, Keeley and Paisley," Joe was saying, however.

Realizing her father was nodding in her direction as he introduced her to the man, Keeley stepped out of the SUV and smiled as the man with the greenest blue eyes she had ever seen greeted, "Welcome to Snow Creek, Keeley." His voice was deep and comforting—just like a hearth fire on a cold night—and it caused goose bumps to tickle the back of Keeley's neck.

"I'm Paisley, and neither one of us is married, by the way," Paisley announced as she followed Keeley out of the SUV.

Boom-Boom-Foxy smiled, exhibiting his perfectly straight pearly whites via his stunning smile once more.

"Well, that's sure good to know," he chuckled. Hunkering down so he was eye level with Paisley, he said, "I'm Sutter Price. And you're gonna have a great time here, Paisley. I promise."

Keeley grinned as she watched Paisley's cheeks pink up with delight. "Oh, I know I will!" she giggled.

Sutter straightened to his full, what must be six-foot-four height and returned his attention to Keeley's father. "Well, why don't you all come into the office, and we'll get your keys so you can head out to your cabin. You guys have the Cozy Cabin, I believe, right?"

"Yep, that'd be us," Joe affirmed.

"Personally, it's my favorite," Sutter offered as he gestured that the family should precede him in heading back into the office. "It's out away from the others...offers more privacy."

"Oh, we know," Cynthia said. "With Joe's family all coming in for the reunion, we need as much privacy as we can possibly get."

"Privacy is a good thing, no matter what, at least to my way of thinking," Sutter agreed.

Oh, the man already had Keeley in the palm of his hand and didn't even know it! He thought privacy was a good thing—something Keeley wholeheartedly believed as well. Yep, she was hooked. Maybe the family reunion for Christmas wouldn't be that bad after all. Not if Sutter Price were part of the package.

Keeley was glad when everyone was finally back in the office. That way, she could enjoy the fine looks of Sutter Price as he talked with her father and typed into the computer at the front desk, and also she didn't have to worry about what she looked like from behind. Keeley hated when men were walking behind her! Of course, she knew true gentlemen always allowed women to precede them. But to Keeley, it was stressful! Once when she'd been a teenager, she'd gone to the movies with a boy she'd been crushing on for over a year. She and her date had shared a box of Goobers during the movie. Although Keeley had thought eating out of the same candy box was romantic as she was doing it, when they left the movie theater later, her date opened the door for her to go first and then started laughing, pointed at her behind, and said, "Ah ha ha! You've got melted chocolate on your butt! It almost looks like you pooped your pants!" Not only was her crush on said boy instantaneously over, she'd been paranoid about walking in front of men ever since!

"Look, Keys!" Paisley said, tugging at Keeley's sleeve.

Disappointed at having to turn her attention from ogling Sutter Price, Keeley turned to see her sister pointing to the fire burning in the hearth on the opposite side of the room.

"Ooo! Doesn't that look warm and cozy, Paiz?" she cooed.

"No, no, no!" Paisley corrected, however. "I mean, yes, the fire looks pretty…but look! There on that coffee table in front of that sofa!"

As understanding immediately hit Keeley, she smiled, responding, "Ooo! A hot chocolate pot and candy canes!"

Indeed, sitting on the large coffee table—in the center of a grouping of very comfortable, rustic furniture arranged to focus on the fireplace—were several wooden serving trays laden with candy canes, plates of cookies, empty mugs, and a large hot chocolate pot.

"Go on over," Sutter said. "And there's plenty more where that came from."

Keeley turned, smiled, and said, "Thank you."

"You bet," he said, winking at her.

She thought she might swoon from the delirium his wink sent drizzling through her. In those moments, Keeley was pretty certain she'd never have a Christmas after that one that offered such winter wonderland eye candy as Sutter Price.

Just as she was pouring hot chocolate into two mugs for her and Paisley, however, the office door burst open.

"Whose idea was it to drive all the way out here for Christmas anyway?" Keeley's aunt Krystal announced as she stepped into the room.

"Yours, Krystal," her aunt Janice reminded as she followed Krystal into the office. Turning and hollering over her shoulder, she added, "Just keep the kids in the car, Dwayne. We won't be long."

"Joe!" Krystal exclaimed, throwing her arms wide as she hurried toward Keeley's father. "Big brother! I've missed you so much!"

"I've missed you too, Krys," Keeley's father said.

"Does he mean it?" Paisley asked, this time in a true whisper.

Keeley nodded as she watched her dad hug first one sister and then the other. "He does, Paiz," she answered. "He really does. It's just the stress of getting here that had him kind of grumpy."

"Oh, good. That makes me happy," Paisley sighed as she plopped onto the sofa.

"Me too," Keeley admitted, more to herself than to her sister. "And here you go. Be careful. It really is pretty hot, okay?" she said as she handed Paisley one of the mugs of hot chocolate—an only half-full mug, just in case. It was a very lovely sofa, after all.

As she retrieved the mug she'd poured for herself and turned around, she glanced up in time to see boom-boom-foxy Sutter Price looking at her. He smiled and winked at her again, as if he understood exactly what she was thinking. But she knew that was impossible! No doubt Sutter Price was thinking that Keeley was a little rattled by the rather boisterous arrival of her aunts. And if it hadn't been the very first day she'd met him, he'd have read her thoughts correctly. But on this occasion, Keeley wasn't thinking of how a family reunion might dampen her Christmas spirit; she was thinking that she wished St. Nicholas really were still alive so that he could bring her Sutter Boom-Boom-Foxy Price as her boyfriend.

CHAPTER TWO

As Keeley sat on the back porch of Snow Creek's Cozy Cabin, she held the steaming mug of hot chocolate close to her face. The moisture of the steam felt so good on her nose and cheeks, and the beloved aroma of simmered cocoa, sugar, and vanilla breathed warmth through her entire body as she inhaled it.

She was so thankful her father had managed to procure the Cozy Cabin for them. When they had been in the office checking in, Keeley had thought the office couldn't get any more crowded and noisy—as Aunt Krystal and Aunt Janice had arrived, none too delicately, as it happened—as they had quickly been joined by Krystal's husband, Tony, Joe's youngest sister, Bev, her husband, Glen, and their three exuberant teenager daughters, Keeley's cousins Debbie, Tiffany, and Molly. But soon it was obvious Uncle Dwayne had decided not to follow his wife's advice and keep the kids in the car, for it was a mere matter of minutes before her cousins Matthew, Corey, Anthony, and Justine joined the group. Janice and Dwayne's kids were a mixture of ages—Matthew and Corey both in their early twenties and Anthony and Justine only a year apart and suffering through the awkward *tween*ager years.

However, through it all, Keeley had managed to stay fairly calm and unirked. That was, until her cousins Ricky and Ethan (Krystal and Tony's boys) waltzed in to join the chaos, as well. Oh, it wasn't that Keeley didn't love Ricky and Ethan; she did. In fact, most of the time she was growing up, Ricky and Ethan had been her favorite cousins of all. Both boys were close to her own age and had lived nearby when they were children. So it wasn't the fact that Ricky and Ethan were there; it was the fact that Ethan had brought a guest—his best friend, Judd.

Ethan had been trying to get Keeley to fall for Judd Sutherland for more than three years! But no matter what she told her well-meaning cousin—no matter how many times she said, "Ethan, Judd is a nice guy, but I'm just not interested"—Ethan and Judd continued to push.

It wasn't that Judd wasn't a nice guy—he was. And he was really good-looking too. Judd was tall, with brilliant blue eyes and sandy blond hair. He was well built and owned a kind, considerate character. But Keeley just wasn't attracted to him—not in any manner whatsoever.

Keeley's mom and dad had not been thrilled to see Judd had accompanied Ethan to the family reunion either. In fact, before Keeley's family had left the office to head to the Cozy Cabin, her father had pulled Krystal aside. Inquiring of his sister as to why on earth a guest had been invited to a Christmas *family* reunion, Keeley's aunt Krystal had simply shrugged and said that Judd had asked Ethan if he could join them and that she and Tony didn't see a problem. After all, Judd had been Ethan's best friend since high school, so what harm could there be in letting him tag along?

"Anyway," Krystal had added in a whisper, "I'm sure Judd's over Keeley by now, Joe. So don't worry."

Joe had immediately glanced to Keeley, and Keeley knew that her father was as irritated with Judd's presence at the *family* reunion as she was. Nevertheless, Keeley knew that, like her, nobody in her family would have ever said anything unwelcoming to Judd—not even an implication or reminder that this holiday was meant to be a family-only reunion. The Joe De Carlo family was nothing if not courteous.

Still, Keeley had felt a lot better when her older brothers, Shane and Alec, arrived with their families. She knew that if Judd did decide to use this opportunity to press her into "getting to know each other better," she could always retreat to either Shane's cabin or Alec's. After all, her brothers were protective of her, and neither Shane's wife, Katelyn, nor Alec's wife, Ariel, thought Judd was a match for Keeley. And besides, both of her brothers had babies—darling little babies that Keeley was dying to cuddle. Shane and Katelyn's son, Luke, was two. Katelyn had nearly wrung Shane's neck the first year after Luke had been born, for Shane never grew tired of saying, "Luke! I am your father," to his baby boy whenever he was holding him. Katelyn eventually quit worrying about it, however, and it never bothered her now. And Luke *did* look just like Shane, after all. Alec and Ariel had a little girl, Jasmine, who was only four months old— still little enough to be in the ideal-for-cuddling category.

Hence, with the arrival of her brothers—and the expressions of disapproval that crossed their faces when they too noted that Judd was there for the long Christmas haul—Keeley figured she had plenty of backup and was able to accompany her parents and Paisley to the Cozy Cabin without too much anticipatory anxiety over Judd taking root in her.

Even so, once they were all settled into the cabin and her mom and dad had convinced Paisley to take a nap while they did, Keeley felt the need for some cool, fresh winter's air and some alone time. And the Cozy Cabin's back porch was just the place to spend it.

Even though the cabin's front porch was wonderful as well, Keeley felt the need to be as invisible to the rest of her relatives as possible. Chances were someone could or would saunter past while taking a stroll or horseback riding. Thus, she'd built a small fire in the fireplace at the far end of the back porch, made a thermos of hot chocolate for herself, settled into one of the soft, comfortable, cushioned porch chairs, propped her feet up on one of the rustic, wooden footstools, and prepared to be alone with her thoughts and relax.

The view from the cabin's back porch was not only tranquil but also spectacular! The pines were so flawlessly flocked with snow that a body would've thought some heavenly artist had hopped down from paradise and personally placed the perfectly precise amount of snow on each needled branch. The cloudless sky was pure azure, and the rocky mountaintops of the far horizon wore their stark white, snowy furs far more majestically than any king had boasted his ermine-trimmed robes.

Fresh snow and frost captured the sunlight, causing the unmarred blanket of white stretched over the ground to sparkle as if it had been sprinkled with a dusting of diamonds—the only sounds the soothing crackle of the fire and Keeley's breath as she occasionally puffed into her mug of hot cocoa to cool it just enough so that it wouldn't burn her tongue.

The wafting scene of burning pine brushed over Keeley's nose, and she smiled, thinking, *Oh, maybe Christmas at the Cozy Cabin won't be so bad.* After all, the proprietors of the cabins at Snow Creek had even provided a beautiful Christmas tree in the Cozy Cabin. Keeley, Paisley, and their mother had been overjoyed when they'd entered the cabin to see a beautiful noble fir tree, strung with soft white mini lights and sequined with gold, ivory, and white glass ornaments.

As they had ooed and awed over the beautiful tree, Keeley's dad had once again proved himself a real man by commenting, "Nice. And I don't even have to help put it away after Christmas."

Keeley's mother had playfully glowered at her husband, but Joe simply shrugged and added, "It's the simple pleasures that make life more enjoyable, babe."

Sipping her cooled-enough-not-to-burn-her-tongue hot chocolate, Keeley grinned as she thought of her parents. She loved her family so very much! And she was truly grateful in that moment, as in every moment of her life, that she'd been born into her father's family via him and not one of his sisters. Oh, she loved her aunts and uncles and cousins, but their mannerisms and lifestyles seemed so loud, hustle-and-bustle, and fatiguing—nothing at all like her own family's. Sure, things came up, and stress was a part of life. But she was so thankful that her dad and mom had always endeavored to make certain their home was a sanctuary from the noise, ugliness, and storms that could be part of the outside world. It had only been recently that Keeley had begun to realize there were valid reasons she required more time to decompress than most others, but she liked to think that her mom and dad had known all along that she, in particular, needed home to be a haven. It was something she'd learned about herself in the book she'd started reading on INFP personality types—her personality type. Keeley was a true INFP—an introvert with deep intuition and the natural ability to feel deeply themselves and tune in to the feelings of others, as well as being a perceiver. Although she'd discovered she was an INFP personality two years before in one of her psychology classes in college, it had taken Keeley awhile to really dive into studying her own personality type—to recognizing her strengths and weaknesses and distinguishing how best to deal with each. It was why the arrival of her extended family at the Snow Creek office had zapped her energy—and why she now felt the need to linger in quiet solitariness for a bit. She had absorbed everyone's energy the moment they entered the room—known exactly who was in a bad mood, who was in a hyperactive mood, who was happy, who was angry—simply by being in the same room with them. And now she needed a reprieve before being in a room with them again.

Keeley sipped her hot cocoa once more. She knew anyone who wasn't familiar with the Myers-Briggs personality type studies would scoff at her—knew they'd tease and make fun of her. And it was why she hadn't mentioned it to anyone other than her mom and dad—probably would never mention it to anyone else in her whole life! A lot of people could be insensitive blockheads sometimes. Still, understanding her personality type had been liberatingly validating to her and educational, as well. And although she would have always sought out peace and quiet after something like the arrival of the whole family all at once in the Snow Creek office, she loved that now she totally understood *why* she had: she needed to recover from the emotionally draining chaotic energy she'd weathered.

As the fire popped a few times as one of the small logs split along a crevice, releasing steam into the fire, Keeley heard a new sound join its steamy exhale—the sound of footsteps crunching through snow.

"Oh no! He's found me!" Keeley thought aloud, wondering if she could bolt back into the cabin before Judd Sutherland saw her.

But when a horse and rider appeared, approaching from the north side of the cabin—when Keeley recognized the barn coat, when she saw that it was Sutter Price who was mounted on the beautiful bay—the desire she had to take flight dissolved.

Holy mackerel! If the guy hadn't already been the hottest boom-boom-foxy man she'd ever seen when he was in the office, the fact he was now riding a horse would've put him there!

Sutter must've heard the fire crackling, because he looked toward the back porch of the Cozy Cabin. Smiling when he caught sight of Keeley, he nodded and said, "Good afternoon there, Miss De Carlo."

"Good afternoon," Keeley called in return.

Her heart leapt as Sutter turned his horse toward her. Dismounting when he'd reached the porch, he haphazardly looped the reins around one of the porch posts and sort of swaggered up the stairs, greeting her with an outstretched, gloved hand as she stood and strode to meet him.

"Was everything ready when you guys got here?" he asked.

Accepting his friendly offer of a handshake, Keeley felt her heart leap again when Sutter grasped her hand, giving it one firm shake.

"Oh, absolutely!" she exclaimed. "And the Christmas tree was such a wonderful surprise too. Thank you for that."

Sutter's gorgeous smile broadened, and he nodded. "Well, some folks who come for the holidays don't care either way whether or not the cabins are festive...but others do."

"Well, I'm one of those who do," Keeley admitted. "So please tell whomever is responsible that I'm grateful."

"I sure will," he assured her.

He stared at her a moment, continuing to smile. Being that Keeley could think of nothing at all to say in an attempt to break the awkward silence and start a conversation with the visual stunner, she was glad when Sutter said, "It's nice out here on the back porch." He winked one of his gorgeous blue-green eyes at her, adding, "The perfect place to escape to, right?"

Giggling a little at his uncanny insight, Keeley affirmed, "I'll admit to not being the most excited about a family reunion for Christmas. But I'm sure it will be a lot of fun."

"Or not," Sutter chuckled with understanding.

Nodding, her own smile broadening then, and she endorsed, "Or not." Then, before the silence could intercede again, she asked, "Would you like some hot chocolate before you head back out? I made a whole thermos-full."

"You bet," Sutter accepted, pulling off his gloves and shoving them into the pockets of his barn coat. "Believe it or not, I never get tired of hot chocolate." Then as Keeley moved to the small standing cabinet to retrieve another mug, he appendixed, "And besides, a guy would be an idiot to refuse a cup of cocoa from a beautiful girl like you."

Even though she blushed to the very tips of her toes—even though she lightly laughed, feigning amusement when in truth she was thoroughly charmed—Keeley teased, "My father is footing the bill for our cabin, mister…so you don't have to butter me up."

"I'm not," Sutter assured her.

Sutter couldn't get over the sensation that there was something exceedingly different about the pretty young woman who was now pouring him a mug of hot chocolate. Sure, she was beautiful— especially standing there in her little fur-lined boots, jeans, very feminine burgundy peplum coat, and ivory crocheted beanie, complete with a crocheted ivory flower on the right side of it. Sutter liked that she wore her shoulder-length brown hair down, so that the beanie pressed it tightly against the sides of her face.

"Thanks," he said as she handed him the mug of hot cocoa. He liked her smile—her friendly, approachable smile. For some reason it gave him the urge to spill his guts to her—tell her his deepest, darkest secrets and see if it marred her opinion of him.

"Wanna sit down and enjoy that?" she asked, motioning to the chair next to the one she'd been sitting in.

"I would," Sutter answered. He plopped down in the chair and propped his feet up on the footstool in front of it. "Ahhhh," he sighed. "I could use a little break."

"Are you riding for fun, or do you have a destination?" Keeley asked.

Sutter looked at her, studying the warm brown of her eyes—soft brown, just like milk chocolate.

"I've got a destination," he admitted. "But it's not too pressing. I just need to head out to the stables and check on the horses…get them fed."

"Oh, wow!" Keeley exclaimed. "Feeding horses. You must love working here."

Sutter nodded, confessing, "I do. It's hard work sometimes, and I don't really enjoy working with the…um…less charming guests. But most of the time it's great out here."

Keeley's pretty eyebrows puckered as she offered, "Gee, I hope my dad's sisters and their families don't end up being in that 'less charming' category. Speaking from experience…it could happen."

Sutter shook his head. "Naw. You're all good people. I can usually tell the moment I meet someone whether or not they're going to be trouble. And you guys are all good."

As if Mr. Murphy were standing right there at that moment, his good ol' law of "if something can go wrong, it will" decided to rear its ugly head.

As Judd Sutherland appeared from around the north corner of the house, exclaiming, "There you are, Keeley! I thought I might find you back here," Keeley's heart sank with a thud to the very bottom, bottom of her stomach.

Not waiting for an invitation, let alone a responding greeting, Judd stepped up onto the porch and asked, "You guys having hot chocolate, or what?"

"Yep," Keeley answered. "Did you want some?" She had to ask—she had to! Her dang courteous nature wouldn't allow her to do otherwise.

"No, thanks," Judd said. "I was just coming by to see if you were busy. And since you are, I'll just head back to the lodge. Ethan and Ricky are there playing foosball in the game room."

"Well, I was just about to—" Sutter began.

Keeley placed her hand on his knee, looking at him and hoping he would understand that she was desperate for him to stay, so that Judd would leave.

"To fill up my mug again, man," Sutter finished. Keeley smiled, hoping he understood she was thankful. "Unless you've changed your mind on having some."

"Nope. I'm good," Judd said.

Judd was smiling in a friendly enough manner. But Keeley knew him pretty well, and he was irritated that he'd found Sutter there with her.

"I'll just head back to the lodge," Judd said. "See you later, Keys." Keeley nodded, and Judd then looked to Sutter. "Enjoy your hot chocolate and your…your ride, I guess," he said, nodding toward the saddled bay horse waiting just off the porch.

"Thanks," Sutter said. "You guys have fun foosballing it up down there. I'd like to get in on that action later, if I could."

"You bet," Judd said, forcing a friendly smile.

"Bye, Judd. Have fun," Keeley called as he descended the porch steps and headed round the south side of the house.

"I will. Thanks," he called over his shoulder.

Once the crunching of Judd's retreating steps in the snow indicated he was out of earshot, Sutter looked to Keeley, grinned, and said, "I take it he's either your least favorite cousin…or not your cousin at all and you're not interested."

"I'm sorry," Keeley said, blushing with the humiliation that had replaced the desperation that had caused her to silently beg Sutter not to leave her alone with Judd.

Sutter grinned and said, "No problem," before taking a swig of his hot chocolate. "I take it that guy isn't your cousin?"

Exhaling a sigh of frustration, Keeley affirmed, "Nope. Though I wish he were. Then there'd never be a reason for my cousin Ethan to keep trying to push me toward Judd."

"So you've got a matchmaker in the family, huh?" Sutter chuckled.

Somehow, the way he put it, it did seem amusing—the fact that her cousin was trying to hook her up, and so stubbornly.

"I guess we do," she said. "And I don't know why Ethan has chosen me to terrorize about it." Keeley paused for a moment, musing. "Maybe it's because I'm not a social butterfly, you know? Maybe Ethan doesn't understand that it's okay to be a loner…and that when *I* find someone whom I find interesting…" She shrugged. "It'll all work out when I want it to and with whom."

"With whom," Sutter repeated. "Wow. Are you a schoolteacher or something?"

Keeley laughed. As much as she loved children, she knew she'd never have the endurance to be a schoolteacher. She'd love the children too much, and every year when her class changed, she'd be devastated. It was cute that he thought she was a schoolteacher simply because she'd used the word *whom* though.

"Nope," she answered. "Nothing as exciting as that. In fact, my job is about as opposite from teaching as it can get. I'm a ghostwriter for several bloggers and columnists. I fill in the blanks when one of them gets stuck or takes a vacation…things like that."

"Wow!" Sutter exclaimed, obviously astonished. "I didn't know there were still ghostwriters around these days. Do you stick strictly to shorter things? Or do you dabble in novels too?"

Keeley felt her cheeks pink with mild embarrassment. "No novels…not yet," she answered. "But I dabble in poetry." She shrugged, adding, "But the kind of poetry I write is…well, let's just say, people nowadays don't have the attention span to read anything too long…or anything that's not dark and depressing for that matter."

"So you write, like…happy stuff?" he asked.

Keeley could see the sincerity on his face. He wasn't mocking her or being sarcastic. His curiosity was genuine.

"Yeah, that's a good way to put it," she confirmed. Keeley never liked the attention of anyone or anything to linger on her life too long. Thus she turned the tables a bit. "But what about you? You must love working here! How great is it to wake up to the quiet of the woods instead of the noise of the city every morning?"

Sutter smiled as he gazed out across the vista before them to the mountains beyond. "Really great, to be honest. I've only been here about a year, and there are a lot of headaches about running a place like this. Of course, any time your business deals with people, you run the risk of headaches." He looked back to Keeley, and she thought she might melt under the warm intensity of his gaze. "I'm sure you know what I mean. Even though you ghostwrite, you still have to deal with your clients, right?"

"Oh yes," she said, knowing exactly what he meant.

"So you know what I mean," he continued. "You have the nice people—like you and your folks." He winked at her, and Keeley giggled a little, pleased by his natural charm. "And then you have the folks who aren't so easy. The towels in their cabin aren't soft enough or the right color; they've never ridden a horse but yell at you when they're sore after a ride. Any form of customer service can be a real...pain in the neck."

"Oh, I hear you," Keeley agreed. "I couldn't do this. I couldn't handle all the strangers and stuff...be responsible for making sure everyone is comfortable."

"I couldn't do it either...not alone, anyway," Sutter offered. "But I grew up here, and I love this place. I dread the day that we have to close it and sell off any more of the property. This was once a working cattle ranch. In fact, I lived here until I left home for college."

"You grew up here? When it was still a ranch?" Keeley asked. Sutter's already infinite attractiveness had just become more infinite! No wonder he sat a horse so perfectly! He'd been a modern-day, real farm-kid-slash-cowboy.

"Yeah," he answered. "It was getting hard to maintain the ranch even before I left home, even though my brothers stayed and worked it for a few years. In the end, we had to sell off about three thousand acres just to have the hope of keeping the other three thousand and being able to keep the cabins at Snow Creek going."

"So you don't just work here. You have a vested interest, at least emotionally, because your family owns this place," Keeley said as the tumblers in her brain fell into place.

Sutter took another swig of hot chocolate. Nodding, he confirmed, "Yep. I certainly do have a vested interest. I would hate to have to see my family let this go. It's like heaven to me."

"Me too," Keeley said—for she really did feel his love for the place. It was in his expression, in the energy she felt from him when he spoke about it.

"But enough about me," Sutter said, smiling at her again. "What can I do to make your Christmas stay here at Snow Creek more enjoyable, hmmm?"

Marry me? Keeley thought to herself.

But out loud she answered, "Oh, this place is perfect! Really!" She shrugged. "I'm just…you know…I kind of like my privacy, my alone time to think and stuff. I'll manage to sneak away here and there. So no worries. I'll be your happiest customer." She smiled at him, adding, "I promise."

Sutter chuckled. "Or at least you'll pretend to be, right?"

The man's insightful intuition was just another thing about him that deserved admiration. She didn't want him thinking she wasn't enjoying herself at his family's property and business, however, so she added, "No, I'm serious. It's so beautiful here! Anyone would be an idiot not to be captivated by it all. I love it!"

Keeley watched as Sutter drained the rest of the hot chocolate from his mug. Setting the mug down on the footstool as he stood up, he said, "Well, I'll tell you what. We have an empty cabin that we keep unreserved for…well, for various purposes. The fridge is fully stocked, and there's even a Christmas tree set up in there. It's small, just one bedroom, a bathroom, a small kitchen, and of course a cozy den. How about, after I've fed the horses, I drop the key off to you? That way, if you find you're ready to tear your hair out because you're so desperate for some solitude, you can just head over there.

It'll be our little secret. I won't breathe a word to anyone. What do you think?"

Well, of course Keeley wanted to jump up from her seat and shout, *Yes! Yes! Yes!!!!* But instead, she simply stood up and said, "Oh no, no, I'll be fine. Gosh, I must have really come across as a whiner just now. I'm sorry, I just—"

"No, not at all," Sutter interjected. "Let's just say I've stood in your shoes one too many times not to know that sometimes an escape hatch saves your sanity. Anyway, it looks like your non-cousin, Judd, isn't going to be too easily deterred. So don't you think you'd like to have the key to the little cabin? It's closer to the main lodge, of course, but if nobody knows it's you in there, it should be private enough."

Keeley could see by the simmer in his downright seductive gaze that he really did know how important a little alone-time could be. Especially in situations like hers.

Just then, the back door to the Cozy Cabin burst open to reveal a very revived-looking Paisley. Not that she had been at all sleepy, tired, lethargic, or cranky before. But now she looked ready to take on the world.

"Hi, Sutter," Paisley greeted with a squeaky voice that revealed to Keeley that her little sister really did think Sutter was boom-boom-foxy. "What're you doin' here?"

Sutter smiled, hunkered down in front of Paisley, and reached out, tweaking her nose. "I'm on my way to feed the horses."

"Ooo! Can I come with you?" Paisley begged.

"Paiz," Keeley kindly scolded, "Mr. Price has work to do, and I've already kept him from it too long, so now he'll have to hurry."

"Aw, shucks," Paisley whined.

Standing erect, Sutter removed his gloves from the pockets of his barn coat. As he pulled them on, he said, "I'll tell you what, Paisley. How about I come by this evening right before bedtime and take you and your big sister on a sleigh ride, hmmm?"

Paisley gasped with instant excitement. "Is it a one-horse open sleigh?"

Sutter smiled, chuckled, and answered, "It is, in fact, a one-horse open sleigh. So what do you say?"

"Oh, please can we go, Keys?" Paisley begged. "I'm sure Dad and Mom won't mind…as long as we do it after the big family dinner!" Looking back to Sutter, she said, "My bedtime is eight thirty. So what time should you be here?"

Sutter laughed as he strode down the porch steps to his horse. After mounting the bay, he said, "How about seven thirty then? You see if your folks think it's okay, and call the office and leave me a message if it's not. Otherwise, I'll see you ladies at seven thirty."

"I'll ask Dad as soon as he's up from his nap!" Paisley squealed.

Keeley was certain that the high-pitched squeal of delight that had trilled from Paisley's throat had just ensured that their father would be up any minute.

Her manners and tendency to want to please others prompted Keeley to want to say, *You really don't have to do that, Sutter.*

However, her madly pounding heart won over the prompting contest, and she said, "Thank you so much, Sutter. I can't imagine how fun a sleigh ride will be."

"Any time," Sutter said. "And anyway, I've got a key to deliver, don't I?" He winked at Keeley and said, "Bye now. You girls have a nice evening."

"Bye," Keeley and Paisley chimed in unison.

Keeley watched Sutter ride away until he turned south and she could no longer see him.

"He really melts my butter!" Paisley said in the alternate voice she'd created after hearing a video clip featuring Holly Hunter and Mae West.

"Paiz! You don't even know what that means!" Keeley scolded, giggling.

"Yes, I do," Paisley argued, however. "It means he makes me feel all warm and buttery inside...like I'm eating a big bowl of hot popcorn with real melted butter all over it."

Keeley didn't know whether to laugh or gasp with astonishment. But in the end, she laughed—for she'd learned long ago that her baby sister's thought processes were far beyond those of other kids her age.

"Well, he melts my butter too," Keeley admitted in her best Holly Hunter impersonation, thinking how perfect Paisley's analogy was. It was true! Even the thought of seeing Sutter Price again caused Keeley to feel all warm and delicious inside—just like a bowl of hot popcorn with melted butter drizzled over it.

CHAPTER THREE

Keeley did her best to focus on enjoying time with her extended family during the family dinner that night. The food was incredible—warm breads, good beef, veggies, just delicious!—not to mention that the Christmas décor in the dining hall of the main lodge was phenomenal. Fresh pine boughs strung with white lights and embellished with red berries and pinecones were draped along the top of each wall, as well as cascading over the railing of the staircase that led to the second story. A large Christmas tree in one corner boasted red and gold ornaments, and a beautiful fire crackled and popped in the large fireplace. Various glass votives and bowls nestled amidst sprigs of fresh holly lined the center of the dining table, each vessel boasting a real candle, each flickering flame lending a sense of magic to the already dazzling room. Keeley was also impressed with the background music those who had arranged the event had chosen—Beegie Adair, her smooth Christmas jazz piano featuring various horns now and then; it was the icing on the perfect holiday dining ambiance.

As for the family itself—Keeley's parents and siblings, the aunts and uncles and cousins—everyone was kind and jovial, sharing fun memories of the past, laughing, and generally having a great time. Of course, the presence of Judd Sutherland did keep Keeley from being truly carefree. Still, she was glad he'd only attempted to sequester her attention three times during the evening, instead of hanging around next to her constantly like he usually did when they were sharing the same airspace. Thus, all in all, the evening was a pleasant one.

Nonetheless, no matter how hard Keeley tried to live in and enjoy the moment, she just kept wishing it were over so that she and Paisley could go on a sleigh ride with Sutter. Therefore, when Sutter entered the lodge in order to add wood to the fire burning in the fireplace at about seven p.m., Keeley couldn't wait any longer! She wanted to be with him, enjoy his company as soon as possible. Oh, she knew it was ridiculous. After all, from what she'd heard from a few of her friends, some people who went looking for love at bars and nightclubs often spent more time with their new, romantic prey—strangers at that—than Keeley had with Sutter. It was weird— she knew it was—the fact that she was so smitten by him, already so obsessed with getting to know him better and spending time with him. The fact was, the whole situation was really not at all like Keeley. And of course, that fact alone made her more curious about Sutter Price—caused her to have a bit more courage than she normally would have. It was why she mustered up the nerve to approach him as he stoked the fire.

"Um…is that offer of a sleigh ride still on the table?" Keeley asked.

"Of course!" Sutter assured her with a smile as he hunkered down in front of the enormous hearth and used a poker to push the new wood into place. "Whenever you're ready. I've got the horse all hitched up and ready to go." His smile broadened as he stood once more, gazing down at her.

Keeley was so mesmerized by the reflection of the fire in his gorgeous eyes that she didn't respond right away.

"In fact...um..." he stammered, shrugging, "if you and your sister have your hats, coats, and gloves here, I can pick you up right outside in, say...five minutes?"

Keeley smiled—felt herself exhale a quiet sigh of enchantment. "We do, and that would be perfect," she said. Suddenly remembering Judd, she added, "But...but would you mind if we kept this kind of...you know..."

"On the down low?" Sutter finished, winking at her. "You mean, so your would-be boyfriend back there—the one who's standing behind you glaring at me like he wants to spit in my Kool-Aid—doesn't want to go with us?"

Keeley giggled quietly, pleased that Sutter was so obviously insightful. "Yeah," she admitted. "I mean, I don't want you to think I'm a jerk or anything..."

"Well, unfortunately the sleigh only seats three people," Sutter offered. "Really only two...comfortably anyway. But your little sister is so small it won't matter." He shrugged, feigning an expression of regret at not being able to fit Judd in the sleigh too. "So you see, we just can't take him with us, I'm afraid."

"Well, shucks," Keeley sighed.

"So...I'll meet you out front in five minutes," Sutter confirmed.

"Definitely!" Keeley quietly exclaimed.

Sutter smiled and winked at her before turning and striding toward the back of the lodge. Keeley could not tear her gaze away from him—away from the way his shoulders dipped and rose as he walked—from the pure, unintentional coolness of his saunter.

"I think he likes you," Judd said from behind her.

Instantly irritated, Keeley gritted her teeth and pasted on a friendly smile before turning to face him.

"He's just offering kind customer service, Judd," she said. "You know that."

"Do I?" Judd mumbled, frowning.

"Well, I would certainly hope so," Keeley playfully exclaimed, "being that you are in the customer service business yourself."

"Hmmm," Judd hummed, only slightly more convinced. "And anyway, I'm not in the customer service business. I'm in financial management."

"Yes," Keeley said, trying to appear calm—trying to mask the fact that she felt like telling Judd to go jump in a lake. "But…if you don't treat your customers—"

"My clients," he interrupted to correct her.

"Yes. If you didn't treat your clients like they're your favorite person on earth, what would happen then, hmmm?" Keeley countered.

"I see your point," Judd admitted, exhaling a sigh as his ire expired.

"Dinner's over, and it's foosball time," Keeley's brother Alec called as he approached. "You won last time, so it's me and you, man. Let's get to it!"

Keeley looked to Alec as he smiled and winked at her. *Saved by the brother*, she thought.

"Um…yeah…okay," Judd stammered as he looked to Alec, back to Keeley, and then back to Alec, as if he knew that if he left to play foosball, Keeley would run. Which she totally planned to.

"See you later, Keys," Alec said as he and Judd started toward the lodge's game room.

"See you later," Keeley called.

Once Alec and Judd had disappeared into the game room, Keeley spun around and headed to where Paisley sat working a puzzle with Ariel.

"Come on, Paiz," she said, taking her little sister by the hand. "It's time for the sleigh ride!"

"Yay!" Paisley said, leaping to her feet. She looked to her sister-in-law, however, quickly explaining, "We can work on the puzzle some more tomorrow...if that's okay, Ariel."

Ariel smiled, her bright green eyes glistening in the low light of the lodge. "You bet, sweetie. You run along and have fun, okay?"

"Thanks!" Paisley said as she sprinted for the coat rack near the front door.

"She's so excited," Ariel noted, smiling at Keeley.

"Well, it is a one-horse open sleigh, from what I understand," Keeley explained. "It's like every child's dream come true...including mine!"

"I'll bet," Ariel said with a wink. "Although I'm not sure whether it's the horse-drawn sleigh or the driver of the horse-drawn sleigh that has put that twinkle in your eyes, Keys," she teased.

"I'll admit to it being both," Keeley said in a lowered voice. "I just hope Alec can beat Judd in foosball a couple of times to keep him from noticing that I've snuck out."

Ariel giggled softly. "Oh, I'm sure he'll do his best," she assured. "Alec was so ticked off when he saw Ethan had brought Judd. How aggravating for you!"

"Yeah," Keeley agreed. "But I'll just be sure to keep busy and—I don't know—hide out as much as I can."

"That's not fair though," Ariel offered. "I mean, it's a family reunion. You shouldn't have to do that. You should be able to enjoy your time with the family."

Keeley shrugged. "I know," she agreed. "But then again…if I'm offered another sleigh ride or two, it'll be worth having to avoid Judd the rest of the time."

Ariel giggled again. "Oh, I have no doubt of that. Have fun, okay? We'll all run interference for you."

"Thanks," Keeley said, sincerely grateful.

"Come on, Keys!" Paisley called in a loud whisper. "I want to sing 'Jingle Bells' while we're riding in the sleigh! Come on!"

Keeley laughed as they hurried toward the coatrack.

"What a great idea, Paiz!" she exclaimed as she pulled on her coat. "Singing 'Jingle Bells' while actually riding in a one-horse open sleigh will be like a dream come true, won't it?"

"Oh, it will!" Paisley giggled. "I can't wait."

Once Keeley had her own coat, hat, scarf, and gloves on, she helped Paisley finish getting hers on.

Just as she was finishing wrapping Paisley's scarf around her tiny, little neck, Paisley gasped and excitedly whispered, "Listen! Keys! Do you hear that?"

"What?" Keeley asked, delighted by her little sister's expression of pure enchantment.

"Listen! I hear bells!" Paisley whispered in awe.

As Paisley's eyes widened with wonderment, Keeley did hear the bells—the rhythmic jingle of sleigh bells.

Pressing her face to a window near the lodge's front entrance, Paisley said, "He's here! He's here! We're really going on a sleigh ride! We really, truly are!"

Keeley was sure her own exuberance matched Paisley's as she opened the lodge door and saw Sutter Price striding toward her—a pearly white, dazzling smile of gorgeousness on his face.

"You ladies ready?" Sutter asked as Keeley and Paisley stepped out of the lodge.

"We are!" Paisley chirped as Keeley closed the door behind them.

"Good," Sutter chuckled as Paisley skipped to him, taking one of his hands with her own.

"Come on, Keys," Paisley called over her shoulder as she pulled Sutter toward the waiting horse and sleigh.

The sleigh itself was beautiful! It was either truly an antique or a fabulous reproduction. The sleigh was red with gold trim, with what looked to be black fur laid over the seats. The horse was a beautiful black gelding, a wide strap of beautiful brass bells encircling its middle.

Goose bumps broke over Keeley's arms and legs as she watched Sutter lift Paisley into the sleigh. He was so handsome, so capable, such a throwback to what masculinity used to be! Once he'd settled Paisley, Sutter turned and offered a hand to Keeley.

"You ready?" he asked as Keeley took his hand and allowed him to help her into the sleigh.

"You have no idea!" Keeley giggled as a joy in the season washed over her.

Sutter chuckled as he stepped into the sleigh and sat down, sandwiching Paisley between himself and Keeley.

"Giddyup, Stackhouse," Sutter said, and the sleigh lurched forward.

Keeley closed her eyes a moment, savoring the sound of the sleigh bells, their perfect rhythm as Stackhouse pulled the sleigh.

The air was cold and crisp, and the only scents Keeley could discern were those of cedar wood burning, leather, and fresh, unsullied air.

"I think Jack Frost is already snipping at my nose," Paisley said.

Keeley opened her eyes and looked over to see Paisley place a warm glove over her nose.

"Oh, he likes to do that," Sutter offered, "especially at night. But you'll warm up soon enough, so don't worry, okay?"

"I'm not worried," Paisley assured him. Keeley could see that Paisley absolutely was not worried—not about her cold nose or anything else in the world. The expression on her pretty little face was that of pure glee.

Keeley felt Paisley's small elbow nudge her ribcage.

"What?" Keeley asked.

"Ask him if we can sing it," Paisley whispered.

"Why don't you ask him?" Keeley whispered in return. She wasn't sure why, but she'd suddenly developed a case of bashfulness. She even felt herself blush when she glanced up at Sutter to see him smiling at her.

"What is it you want to ask me?" he offered, alleviating both Keeley and Paisley of their momentary tentativeness.

"I…well, you see…" Paisley stammered. "It just seems like we should sing it, you know? Since we're riding in a one-horse open sleigh and stuff."

Sutter chuckled. "You mean we should sing 'Jingle Bells'?"

"Yeah," Paisley admitted.

"But if it's a problem or it will bother the horse or something…" Keeley began.

"Not at all," Sutter assured her. "In fact, I'd say Stackhouse might not think he's doing a good job if we don't sing it at least once."

Sutter winked at Keeley as Paisley exclaimed, "Oh, yay! I'm so excited!"

"Do you want to start us off?" he inquired of Paisley.

Without hesitation, Paisley began, "Dashing through the snow…in a one-horse open sleigh…"

Keeley's heart leapt as Sutter's low, masculine, and downright fabulous singing voice joined in, *"O'er the fields we go…laughing all the way!"*

"Bells on bobtails ring, making spirits bright…" Keeley merged.

"Oh, what fun it is to ride and sing a sleighing song tonight!" the three sleigh passengers sang in unison.

Keeley was absolutely enraptured by the moment—by the evening—by the man driving the sleigh! Everything seemed as if it had been coaxed into stepping directly out of a Currier and Ives print. The atmosphere was ethereal, and Keeley wondered for a moment if she were just dreaming up Sutter Price—feared she might wake up and find Judd Sutherland driving the horse instead of the exquisite specimen of handsome manliness she was singing "Jingle Bells" with.

"That was so fun!" Paisley giggled once the song had ended. "I'm so glad someone invented 'Jingle Bells' for people to sing to them."

"Do you know why bells were first put on horses when they were pulling sleighs?" Sutter asked Paisley.

Paisley shrugged. "Um…because they sound pretty?"

Sutter smiled and, without implying that Paisley's guess had been altogether wrong, offered, "They do sound pretty, don't they? And that sound lets other sleighs know that someone is nearby so the horses and sleighs don't collide."

"Ohhhh," Paisley responded.

"See how dark it is now that we're away from the cabins?" Sutter continued. "Well, back in the olden days, there wasn't even that much light to guide people when they were out for a sleigh ride. And notice that the horse and sleigh don't make much noise either. So folks started putting bells on their horses so other folks could hear them driving in the dark. Everybody's bells sounded different too. So let's say your dad was coming home from somewhere, and he was driving his sleigh…"

"Yeah…" Paisley prodded.

"Well, if you heard sleigh bells passing near to your house, you would be able to run outside, stay very still, and listen," Sutter explained. "And you would know if it was your dad coming home or just a neighbor driving by, because you would've become accustomed to the way everybody's sleigh bells sounded, especially your dad's. Does that make sense?"

Paisley nodded. Keeley watched as Paisley put her arms around one of Sutter's and hugged him, nuzzling against his coat.

"I like your sleigh bells, Sutter," she sighed. "I will never forget just how your sleigh bells sound. I promise."

Keeley watched as Sutter's smile—his entire expression—turned to that of gratitude and contentment.

"Well, I hope not," he said.

The trio rode in silence for a time, and Keeley knew that her little sister was as entranced as she was by the rhythmic sound of the bells and the smooth crunch of the snow as the sleigh cut through it.

After a while—once they were quite a ways out from the cabins—Sutter suggested, "Hey, Paisley, why don't you drive for a while?"

"What?" Keeley squeaked the same moment that Paisley exclaimed, "Really?"

He puffed a quiet laugh, winking at Keeley with reassurance.

"Sure," he answered, offering the reins to Paisley.

Paisley took the reins like she was a fox who had been starving for a moment and was about to have a turkey dinner.

"You want to go straight," Sutter instructed. "So don't pull back on them, or he'll stop. Just keep them in your hands, and don't pull on one harder than the other."

"I won't," Paisley assured him.

Keeley smiled as she watched her little sister's brows knit together on her forehead. The poor thing was concentrating with all her might!

"You can relax," Sutter said. "Stackhouse knows what he's doing. As long as you keep the reins in your hands without letting them go too slack, he'll just keep going straight until we tell him otherwise, okay? I want you to have fun…so just relax."

Sutter reached down and retrieved first one small travel thermos from under his seat and then another.

"You drive for a bit, okay, Paisley?" he asked. "That way Keeley and I can enjoy our hot chocolate. And when we're finished, you can let Keeley take over, and you can enjoy yours, okay?"

"You brought us hot chocolate?" Paisley chirped with delight.

"Of course," Sutter assured her. As he handed one of the small thermoses to Keeley, he said, "I wouldn't bring you on your first sleigh ride and forget the hot chocolate."

"Thanks," Keeley said as she accepted the thermos. "For everything," she added.

"You bet," Sutter said with a wink.

"Can we sing another Christmas song?" Paisley asked, straightening in her seat with pride in knowing she was driving the horse.

"Of course. Why don't you choose another one for us?" Sutter said just before he took a sip of his hot chocolate.

"Let me see." Paisley mused. And almost immediately she began to sing, "*Good King Wince's snot froze up, on his way to Steven's.*"

The discomfort Keeley felt when she snuffed her own sip of hot chocolate into her sinuses was miserable. But Sutter spewing his own mouthful of hot chocolate over Stackhouse's rump was so funny, she laughed instead of cried as hot chocolate dribbled from her nose.

Nevertheless, there was no rest for the amused. As Keeley dabbed at her nose with the back of her glove and Sutter wiped his mouth with the back of his, Paisley was in her glory and undaunted.

"And some folks laid all about, then they kissed at Steven's," she continued to sing. "Brightly shone the sun that night, so Jack Frost was cool. Then a doorman came inside, gathering people's stool."

By now, Keeley was trying so hard to restrain laughter that she thought she might explode! For his part, Sutter was hanging over the side of the sleigh attempting to muffle his own.

Paisley, as was often the case, was clueless. "Oh, I just love that song," she sighed. "I should probably learn the other parts someday...but it's a long song, you know."

"I do know," Sutter said, straightening in his seat and wiping mirthful moisture from the corners of his eyes.

Keeley was even further impressed by Sutter's sense of humor and also his willingness to keep the fact that Paisley had slayed the beloved carol to himself. She sighed, brushing away her own tears of amusement. As she gazed at Sutter, still smiling with lingering merriment, something inside her suddenly welled with such powerful and unexpected force, it literally took her breath away. She'd known Sutter mere hours, and yet she felt drawn to him in every respect— not just physically because of his attractiveness but emotionally, soulfully—as if everything that was her was trying to tell her something, trying to advise her, promising her that Sutter Price was meant to change her life.

"Do you want to sing another song?" Sutter asked Paisley.

But Paisley yawned, shaking her head. "Nope. I feel like having my hot chocolate now and letting somebody else drive Stackhouse," she answered. "Whew! I had no idea how hard horse driving is!"

"It does wear a person out here and there," Sutter agreed, putting his thermos down and taking the reins when Paisley offered them to him. "In fact, we probably oughta get you girls home. Didn't you tell me your bedtime is at eight thirty?"

"Yeah," Paisley yawned. "Keeley doesn't have to go to bed as early as I do because she's finished growing." All at once Paisley's eyes widened, and a worried expression puckered her brow. "But…but can we go sleighing another time? Me and Keeley and you, Sutter? Stackhouse too, of course."

"You bet we can," Sutter assured Paisley with a wink. He reached down near his feet and produced another small thermos. "Here you go," he said, handing Paisley her hot chocolate. "I'll get Stackhouse headed back to the cabins so you can get warmed up and get to bed, okay?"

Paisley nodded, flipped the little lid of the thermos open, and sipped her hot chocolate.

"So…um…you have a later bedtime than your sister, do you?" Sutter asked, glancing to Keeley.

"Indeed I do," Keeley answered, suddenly hopeful. Maybe he would invite her to have some more hot chocolate or to enjoy a fire on the Cozy Cabin's back porch. Biting the inside of her cheek in attempting to hide her hope that Sutter had a reason, other than casual conversation, for asking her about her bedtime, Keeley held her breath.

"Well, to be honest, this is about the shortest sleigh ride I've ever taken anyone on," Sutter confessed. "And I'm sure Stackhouse would like to be out a bit longer. So…if you don't have family reunion plans, do you…wanna go on another wintery sleigh ride with me after we drop Paisley off?"

"Oh, I would love it!" Keeley managed to answer without jumping up and down with elation.

"Good," Sutter said, exhaling a heavy sigh, as if he'd been holding his breath too.

"This is the best hot chocolate I've ever had!" Paisley exclaimed. "I don't understand why you spit yours out, Sutter. Was it too hot for you?"

Keeley giggled, and Sutter chuckled, "Yep. I guess I should've cooled it off a bit first, huh?"

"Yeah," Paisley agreed. "You need to be careful or you'll burn your tongue, you know."

"That's true," Sutter agreed.

Frowning again, Paisley looked up to Keeley. "Keys…you haven't hardly said anything this whole trip. Are you feeling okay?"

Keeley smiled at her little sister, put an arm around her shoulders, and pulled her close.

"Oh, I'm feeling great, Paiz," she answered. "I suppose I'm just enjoying the beauty of the night." Then looking to Sutter, she blushed a little as she added, "And the company, of course."

"Well, maybe I've missed something," Paisley said. "Maybe we shouldn't sing on the way home. Maybe I'll just listen to the bells."

"Oh, that sounds nice," Keeley said. She could see Paisley was getting sleepy. And the hot chocolate would just contribute further to her lethargy. Keeley wouldn't be surprised if Paisley was asleep in the mere fifteen or so minutes it would take to get back to the Cozy Cabin.

Something flew over them then. Something that—though unseen—felt big.

"What was that?" Paisley asked. "A giant bat?"

But Sutter shook his head. "Nope. That was an owl. I didn't see it that time, but it was probably a great horned owl. We have a few really big ones living near here."

"Oh, I've always loved owls," Keeley commented. "It's been so long since I've seen one. But I mostly love them calling…especially at night. Are there any that live close enough to the cabin area that we might hear them?"

"Oh, great. Now she'll never stop talking," Paisley sighed. "Keeley loves nature stuff."

Sutter smiled. "We sure do. I hear a couple of great horned owls hooting every night. And a snowy owl here and there."

Keeley was delighted! To her, owl calls were one of the most soothing night sounds she'd ever heard. Not that she'd heard them very often—mostly when she was younger on family trips to Yellowstone or some other place for camping. But she'd visited a friend who lived just outside of Seattle the autumn before and had drifted off to sleep to the soothing hoots of owls every night she was there.

"Oh, how fun!" Keeley breathed. "I love hearing them." She looked to Sutter, adding, "This place of yours just keeps getting better and better."

"Well, I'm glad it's growing on you," Sutter said with a wink.

Just then, Keeley did indeed hear an owl hooting in the not-too-far-off distance. Even over the sleigh bells she heard it, and it sent a feeling of pure contentment drizzling through her.

"If you have time and are at all interested," Sutter began, "I can take you owling one night."

"Owling?" Keeley asked.

"Yeah," Sutter affirmed. "We'd have to do it pretty late, around midnight or just before. We just walk out into the woods—quietly, of course—and then we try to call for an owl and see if we can coax one our way."

Goose bumps of anticipatory delight erupted over Keeley's arms.

"Are you for real?" she teasingly asked Sutter.

"What do you mean?" he asked, frowning a little.

"I mean…this!" Keeley gestured toward the horse and sleigh bells and then up toward the sky where the owl had flown over them. "Sleigh rides? Jingle bells? Owling? I've never in all my life met a man like you."

Quirking one eyebrow, Sutter said, "I'm hoping that's a compliment…right?"

"Of course!" Keeley giggled. "Why would you think otherwise?"

Sutter shrugged. "You'd be surprised what some people think is weakness and what others don't."

Keeley frowned, a measure of her joy evaporating. There was something in Sutter's demeanor all of a sudden—something sad.

"And it looks like we may have to reschedule your second sleigh ride as well, Miss De Carlo," he said then.

Keeley followed his gaze. They were nearly to the Cozy Cabin, and Keeley's heart sank to the pit of her stomach. For there, sitting in a chair on the front porch, was Judd Sutherland.

She wanted to scream with frustration as she watched Judd rise from his chair, descend the steps of the cabin's front porch, and stare at them. He was waiting for them to arrive—waiting for her to arrive. Keeley wondered how long he'd been waiting. She knew the sleigh ride couldn't have taken more than forty minutes—even though it felt like it had only been ten.

As the sleigh drew closer to the cabin, Keeley saw her mother step out onto the porch. No doubt she was anxious to get Paisley to bed so she could spend some quiet time with Keeley's father.

"Um…I would really like to still go…if you think Stackhouse is up for it," Keeley offered. "If you're still up for it." She was desperate to stay with Sutter—more desperate to stay in his company even than she was to avoid Judd's. Furthermore, she was disturbed by the way Sutter had addressed her as "Miss De Carlo"—as if he was intentionally wedging less familiarity between them.

"I heard the bells!" Cynthia exclaimed, smiling as Sutter pulled Stackhouse to a stop in front of the Cozy Cabin. "They're beautiful, Sutter!"

"Thank you, ma'am," Sutter said, offering a friendly nod and grin.

Just as Keeley had suspected, Paisley was sound asleep in the sleigh, and Sutter hopped down, gathering her in his arms and starting toward the cabin.

"Thank you so much," Cynthia said as Sutter transferred Paisley from the cradle of his arms to the cradle of her mother's. "I hope she wasn't too much trouble."

"She was great," Sutter said. "No worries."

Keeley gritted her teeth as Judd strode to the sleigh and offered her his hand to assist her. Not having it in her to be flat-out rude, even to Judd, Keeley plastered on a smile and took his hand, muttering, "Thank you, Judd."

"I've been waiting for you," Judd said, stating the obvious.

"Well, actually, I was going to go out again with—" Keeley began.

"You all have a good night," Sutter said as he headed back toward the sleigh.

Keeley was furious—furious and heartbroken! Judd was ruining her entire life! Why couldn't he take a hint?

"Thank you, Sutter," Keeley said as Sutter climbed back into the sleigh. "I…I really do wish you would give me a rain check."

"You got it," he said, smiling at last. "Oh! And don't forget your thermos," he added, reaching down and retrieving one of the thermoses he'd brought with him. "It's…uh…complimentary, remember?"

Keeley didn't remember, but she wasn't about to admit it. He was offering her a thermos; to her it would be a souvenir from her very first sleigh ride—a memento of the most fascinating man she'd ever known.

Sutter held out the thermos, and Keeley hurried to him to accept it.

But when he handed it to her, he winked and whispered, "Sorry if I seemed a little terse. I'll admit to you I was bugged to see him waiting for you."

"You were?" Keeley breathed—thoroughly delighted.

"Yeah," Sutter said. "And anyway, I forgot to give you this."

"The complimentary thermos?" Keeley asked.

Sutter chuckled. "No…this."

He opened his other gloved hand, and Keeley smiled when she saw a key lying in his palm.

"I really think you *are* going to need this at some point," he said. "It's to the little cabin just behind the lodge. Use it any time, okay?"

"But…but I…" Keeley stammered. She wanted nothing more than to take the key, but it seemed not only selfish but also like stealing towels from a hotel for some reason.

"Use it any time," Sutter said. Then, as Keeley accepted the thermos with one hand, Sutter pressed the key into her other.

"Giddyup, boy," he instructed Stackhouse. "You folks have a good night, and let me know if you need anything," he said as the sleigh lurched forward.

"Thank you!" Keeley called after him.

She watched him sleigh away—listened to the rhythm of Stackhouse's bells.

"That guy's a total hick, huh," Judd said as he stepped up to stand beside her. "Horses? Beat-up old sleds? Is he stuck in the 1800s or what?"

Keeley gritted her teeth, determined to keep her cool. Judd wasn't a bad guy, after all—just a citified weenie.

"But it was nice that he took Paisley out for some fun," Judd added. He'd almost redeemed himself a bit, until he added, "Nice that he let you go too. Smart actually. He is a stranger after all. It wouldn't do for him to be taking Paisley anywhere by herself."

"Did you want something, Judd?" Keeley asked—a little too curtly to her way of thinking.

"Um…just to see you," Judd answered. It was obvious her briskness had surprised him a bit. "We didn't have much time to talk tonight. So…I thought we could sit out here and watch the frost fall for a while and just…hang."

Keeley looked up to see that, indeed, tiny crystals of frost were drifting down through the cold night air. She hadn't even noticed. In fact, it seemed that the moment she'd seen Judd waiting for her on the porch, all the beauty of the winter wonderland she'd been so acutely aware of and adoring only moments before had vanished. It was as if the beauty of the night, the wonder of the sleigh ride, the laughter she and Sutter had shared over Paisley's "Good King Wince's snot freezing" had ridden away with him.

Still, Sutter had said he'd been bugged by seeing that Judd was waiting for her. He'd given her the key to the empty cabin—the secret key to the empty cabin. He'd also given her a rain check on their sleigh ride together, as well as offering to take her owling. Thus, as Keeley thought it over—even as Judd followed her up onto the front porch—her heart began to rise from the pit of her stomach and back into her chest. Sutter Price wasn't going anywhere any time soon. She'd have another opportunity to bask in his fascinating, alluring company.

"What are you smiling about?" Judd asked, chuckling. "You look like a kid on Christmas morning."

"Just thinking," Keeley said. And she was thinking—thinking about Sutter and the fact that he did make her feel similarly to the way she had felt as a child—a child who still believed in Santa Claus and woke up Christmas morning to find that the "right jolly old elf," who loved all children everywhere, had visited her home during the night, leaving a stocking filled with candy, nuts, and tiny gifts near the hearth and a toy or two under the tree meant just for her.

Keeley giggled as she plopped down on one of the chairs on the porch. She felt better all of a sudden—even felt she could endure a friendly chat with Judd.

"What's so funny?" Judd asked.

"Nothing," Keeley said. But silently to herself, she remembered the joy and excitement she'd owned as a child who still believed—lingered on the joyful sensation of excitement she'd felt that night while sleigh riding with Sutter. "He even drives a sleigh," she whispered to herself, smiling as old Jack Frost nipped at her nose.

CHAPTER FOUR

The sun was white and bright and warming, and the cloudless sky and lack of any breeze made for perfect sledding and tubing weather. As Keeley stood at the top of the hill, one arm propped on a large inflated inner tube, she was glad her aunt Krystal had been the one to plan the first full day of the De Carlo family reunion. While Keeley's aunts Janice and Bev were the true hostess types, overseeing the dinners, party games, and more refined aspects of the reunion, Krystal was her Dad's sister who tended to throw caution to the wind in favor of fun. Therefore, even though her aunt Krystal and uncle Tony's lax parenting was one reason Keeley's cousin Ethan thought it was okay to bring Judd along to a family event, it was also the reason a day of sledding and inner tubing had been planned.

Therefore, Keeley had decided to cut her aunt Krystal some slack over her careless attitude about her son bringing a friend to a family event and just enjoy the warm weather and fun. After all, with Sutter Price in attendance to oversee the excursion—although she figured the liability release forms everyone had to sign before snow-play that morning were his main reason for being there—what wasn't to enjoy?

Sure, it bugged Keeley the way her cousins Debbie, Tiffany, and Molly were so shamelessly flirting with Sutter—giggling like goofy bobbleheads every time Sutter looked their way or assisted them somehow with their tubes. But it was what teenage girls did, and so Keeley brushed it off as best she could and tried to focus on having fun.

"Now, hang on, honey," Keeley's father instructed her mother. Keeley watched as her dad held her mom's inner tube steady while her mom climbed on.

"I will," Keeley's mom said. "It's not like I haven't done this a million times before, Joe."

"I know," Joe affirmed. "But this is a pretty steep slope, so—"

"I've got it," Cynthia giggled. "Now shove me!"

"Okay," Joe said. He bent over then, pushing on Cynthia's tube and sending it sliding down the snowy slope.

Everyone applauded as Cynthia screamed with enjoyment, catapulting down the slope and even catching some air a time or two as the tube blasted over a couple of mounds of snow.

"Good one, babe!" Joe shouted as Cynthia's tube skidded to a stop at the bottom of the hill. "Nice form!" he laughed.

"Will you go with me, Judd?" Keeley heard her little sister ask.

Glancing to where Judd stood almost right next to her, Keeley frowned when Judd patted Paisley on the head and said, "Um…not this time, Paiz. I was thinking I would go with Keeley."

Keeley was furious. What a jerk! Turning down Paisley's request to try and maneuver himself into position to go with Keeley? Oh, Keeley was livid.

Not waiting for assistance and without a word to Judd, Keeley plopped her tube down at the top of the slope. "Look out, Mom!" she called down to her mother. "Incoming!"

"But, Keys—" Judd began as Keeley settled herself on her inner tube and pushed off.

Just as it had been every time before over the past four hours, the steep slope of Snow Creek's tubing area did not disappoint! The wind was cold on her face as Keeley blew down the hill toward the bottom. It cooled her irritation with Judd a little too. And when she hit a hill and went flying off of her tube to land in the soft snow at the bottom, she didn't even care that her shoulder hurt a little—because it had been an epic slide, and it made her laugh.

As she struggled to her feet and looked up at everyone back at the top of the hill, she raised her hand and waved as they all applauded and whistled with approval at her grand wipeout.

"Look out, Keys!" Paisley called then. "We're comin' for you!"

Keeley smiled, her heart swelling with gratitude as she watched Sutter position himself and Paisley on a large tube. She could tell that Sutter was sitting low in the tube with Paisley on his lap. No doubt he was planning to drag his butt a little to keep things less daredevilish for Paisley on their way down.

"Freaking Judd is a douche," Keeley's mom growled as she stood next to Keeley holding her own tube.

"Mom!" Keeley laughed.

But Cynthia De Carlo was still frowning. "Well, that's what your brothers call him…and I agree! I mean, how many times today has Paisley asked him to go down with her? Hmm? Ten? And he's rejected her every time! Not that I *want* my baby in his care at all…but still. I could wring Krystal's neck for letting Ethan bring him! She had to know he was going to try and follow you around like a dork." Cynthia exhaled a heavy sigh and added, "But Sutter is a nice guy. Look at him! You know he's going to burn his butt on the snow to keep them going slow enough for Paiz, that it won't be great fun for him, but he's going to do it."

"I do know," Keeley said as she watched Sutter launch their tube down the hill.

Paisley's squeals of delight were priceless as Sutter hung tight to her as they slid. And when they hit the bottom near where Keeley and her mother stood watching, toppling over into the snow, Paisley burst into giggles as Sutter picked her up and tossed her into a nearby snow drift.

As Sutter offered a hand to Paisley and pulled her up out of the drift, Keeley's smile grew wider and wider. He really was a nice guy. Oh, sure, he had a vested interest in making sure Keeley's family had a good time—all of them. But she could see that the smile on his face was nothing but sincere—that he'd enjoyed taking Paisley down the slope.

"Thanks, Sutter!" Paisley chirped. "That was the best ride I've had all day! Will you take me again? Please?"

Without pause, Sutter reached out, tweaking Paisley's little cherry-red nose and answering, "You bet."

"Mama! Did you see me?" Paisley exclaimed as she hurried to her mother.

"I sure did!" Cynthia laughed, giving Paisley a hug. "Help me drag my tube up the hill, and then you can go again when Sutter has a minute."

"Okay," Paisley agreed. Then running up the hill ahead of her mother, the little girl turned around, waving an arm in gesture that Cynthia should follow her. "Come on, Mom! I can't wait to go again!"

Shaking her head with amusement—and probably fatigue—Keeley's mom looked to Sutter and said, "Thank you so much, Sutter. She gets overlooked a lot during these get-togethers because she's so much younger than everyone else. Thank you for being so kind and patient."

"She's a kick in the pants," Sutter chuckled. "And I enjoyed it too. No worries. I'm happy to do it…really."

"Thanks," Cynthia reiterated. Then, towing her tube behind her with one hand, she began trudging up the hill.

"That really was great, Sutter," Keeley said when Sutter looked at her to find her gazing at him. "Above and beyond the call of duty, for sure."

But Sutter shrugged. "I don't see why," he said. "Stuff like this should always be about the kids. I think people forget that sometimes." He winked at her, adding, "Here, I'll take your tube too," as he reached out and took hold of the rope tied around Keeley's inner tube for more convenient transport.

"Oh, I can take it," Keeley began to protest.

"Oh, I know you can," Sutter agreed. "But I'm trying to make some points with you here, you know?"

Keeley blushed, delighted by his forthright admission and flirting.

"Come on! I'll race you to the top!" he laughed as he took off like a shot up the snowy hill.

"Oh no, you don't!" Keeley laughed as she hurried after him.

"Take your time, Mrs. De Carlo," Sutter said to Keeley's mother as he passed her on his way up. "It's no fun if you have to wear yourself out bringing your tube up. I'll come back down and get yours when these two are up."

"You don't have to do that," Cynthia said. "I'm sure Joe will take pity on me here any minute."

"Sorry, Mom!" Keeley called as she passed her mother in pursuit of Sutter. "But my reputation is at stake here."

"I can see that!" she heard her mother laugh.

Still, as hard as she tried, Sutter did indeed beat her to the crest of the sledding hill.

"No fair," Keeley huffed and puffed when she reached the top as well. "You have bigger muscles than I do!"

"I would hope so," Sutter chuckled as he dropped the tubes.

"Hey, look at this!" Judd shouted, drawing everybody's attention to where he stood across the way to the opposing side of the sledding hill.

Everyone did look—everyone except Keeley's father.

"I better help your mom," Joe said as he started down the sledding hill toward Cynthia.

Keeley smiled, pleased as always with her father's caring attendance to her mother.

"How come we're not sliding down this side, Price?" Judd asked as everyone moved toward where he stood looking down. "This hill is epic, man! Why aren't we using this one instead?"

Keeley watched as Sutter inhaled a deep breath. She could tell he was irritated by Judd and trying to keep his cool.

"It's not safe," was Sutter's simple but firm answer. "There's no way to keep from sliding out onto the lake, and we don't feel the lake has frozen solid enough this year to risk it. Thus, the sign that's posted right there."

Keeley looked down the slope. Yep! There at the bottom was a small lake that appeared to be frozen solid. Yet the fact that no snow was covering the ice of the lake was enough for Keeley to assume that it wasn't frozen as solid as it could be—even with her lack of experience.

"I can stop before I hit the lake," Judd boasted, however.

"No, man, you can't," Sutter told him. "All you'll do is cause a problem and possibly get someone else hurt in the process."

Nevertheless, Judd grumbled, "What do you know, farm boy?"

Keeley was certain that, had Sutter been closer to Judd, he could've reached out and taken ahold of Judd's arm in time to stop him. But Sutter wasn't close enough. Therefore, even though Sutter did lunge at Judd the moment Judd hopped on his inner tube and pushed off, he wasn't able to keep him from taking off down the snowy hill.

"Dammit!" Sutter growled, scowling as he watched Judd slip away down the hill.

"Yeehaw!" Judd shouted as he raced down the icy slope.

Then, just as Sutter had predicted, Judd's tube did not stop at the bottom of the hill but continued to travel out over the surface of the frozen lake.

"Ah ha ha ha!" Judd laughed as he stood up out of his tube. Putting his hands to his mouth, he shouted, "See? I told you it would be fine, farm boy!"

In the very next instant, everyone watching at the top of the hill gasped as the sound of the ice cracking echoed through the small valley that housed the lake. In a second, Judd disappeared beneath the surface of the winter water, bobbing up a moment later and gasping himself—only Judd was gasping for breath.

"Shit!" Sutter exclaimed under his breath as he turned and hurried toward the pickup he'd driven some of the women out to the site in.

"He'll drown!" Krystal screamed.

"That or he'll freeze to death," Tony said.

Debbie, Tiffany, and Molly burst into tears as Alec and Shane followed Sutter to the truck.

"What do we do to help?" Shane asked.

"Just stay up here and hold onto this rope for me," Sutter said, handing a thick wheel of rope to Alec. "You'll probably have to pull him up."

Taking another wheel of rope from the back of the truck, Sutter put one arm through it, securing it on his shoulder as he strode quickly back to the edge of the top of the hill.

"What a dipshidiot," he growled a moment before he leapt off the hill and began sliding on his hip and one elbow down toward the bottom, the lake, and where Judd now was shouting for help.

"Maybe we oughta go with him," Ethan suggested.

"No," Alec answered. "He knows what he's doing. If any of us go, we'll just end up in the lake like Judd."

"Keeley," Paisley said, moving to stand next to Keeley, "will Sutter save Judd?" she whimpered as tears spilled over her cheeks.

Keeley dropped to her knees and drew her little sister into a comforting embrace. "I'm sure he will, Paiz. I'm sure he will."

Keeley felt guilty because her aggravation with Judd and his stupid stunt outweighed her concern for him. Of course, she was concerned for Sutter's safety as well, but somehow she knew Sutter would return unscathed. Judd, on the other hand…

"Dipshidiot? Was that what he said?" Shane asked.

"Yeah, I think so," Alec answered.

"Well, it fits, that's for sure," Shane grumbled.

"Oh, come on now," Ethan began to argue. "Judd didn't intend to end up in the lake."

Everyone looked at Ethan for a moment—frowned at him, actually.

"Sutter's there!" Paisley exclaimed, returning everyone's attention to what was going on at the bottom of the hill.

Of course, Keeley's attention had been fixed on Sutter the whole time. She hadn't even looked away to give Ethan a scolding look the way everyone else had. And now she watched as Sutter adeptly stopped himself before sliding into the lake and leapt to his feet. Swiftly he tied one end of the rope he'd brought with him to a nearby, very large pine tree.

"What's going on?" Keeley's father asked as he and Cynthia arrived on the scene.

"Judd ignored Sutter when Sutter explained why he didn't have us sledding down this hill instead of that one," Keeley's uncle Dwayne explained. "The idiot ended up in the water."

"That kid is an idiot," Joe mumbled.

"We've all come to that same conclusion," Dwayne agreed.

Keeley held her breath as she watched Sutter take hold of the free end of the rope, wrapping it securely around his left wrist as he ventured out onto the ice. She knew it was even more obvious to Sutter than it was to everyone watching that Judd was incapable of making it to the shore alone. In fact, even though Judd tried to pull himself out of the water, the ice either broke more, plunging him back in, or he just slipped.

"Give me your hand!" Sutter shouted. His voice echoed off the walls surrounding the valley.

"I'm too tired," Judd shouted in return.

"Oh no!" Keeley gasped as she watched Sutter tie the rope around his waist, lie down on the ice, and start army-crawling toward Judd.

No one spoke—only watched in anticipation and horror.

"Now…take my hand!" Sutter ordered as he reached Judd.

Judd panicked, however, and, instead of taking hold of Sutter's outstretched hand, reached up and grabbed the back of his jacket, pulling himself up out of the water and onto Sutter's back and sending Sutter plunging headfirst into the icy water.

"Judd!" Keeley screeched with anger and fear. "Help him!"

But Judd just continued to cling to the rope, pulling himself to shore and leaving Sutter gasping for breath when he finally broke the water's surface.

"What a douche," Alec growled.

Sutter managed to pull himself out of the water using the rope all the same, and Keeley nodded with approval as Sutter shoved Judd to the ground when he reached the shore to find Judd standing with his back to Sutter, waving up to everyone standing on the hill.

"Get up!" Sutter barked, removing the rope that was anchored by the pine.

Scowling and dripping wet—also visibly shivering—Sutter looked to the crest of the hill. "Tie the rope off to the hitch on the truck and throw it down here. I doubt he's got the strength to climb up on his own."

"You got it!" Shane and Alec responded in unison.

Keeley watched, thankful that her brothers were both capable men, as Shane tied the rope to the truck's hitch and Alec tossed the remaining length down the hill to Sutter.

Sutter tied the new rope around Judd's waist. "Try to stay on your feet," he said to Judd, the echo reaching to the top of the hill. "It'll be hard enough for them to drag your stupid ass up there if you're walking, let alone if you're nothing but dead weight."

Then looking up to Alec and Shane, Sutter shouted, "Okay! Haul him up!"

Shane and Alec did begin to pull on the rope as Judd somehow managed to remain standing.

Sutter did not run ahead of Judd but stayed behind him, pushing him along and using his own strength to propel them both up the hill.

When they reached the crest, Judd dropped to his knees, shivering uncontrollably—his teeth chattering, his lips blue.

"I gotta get him back right away," Sutter said as he reached to his back, taking hold of his coat and stripping it and his shirt off in one swift move. "We need to get him attended to…warmed up." Everyone stood silent as Sutter then stripped off his thermal underwear shirt and tossed it into the bed of the truck. Opening the truck's passenger side door, he reached behind the seat and retrieved a dry barn coat, but instead of putting it on, he tossed it to Alec, saying, "Get his coat and shirt off, and put that on him."

Reaching back into the pickup, Sutter retrieved a walkie-talkie. "Base…come in. I'm bringing a guest in who is wet and in danger of hypothermia. Please meet me at the office…and send Dad out here to pick up everyone else. Over."

Almost instantly a woman's voice responded. "Roger that, Sutter. I'll send Dad now. I'll be waiting for you to bring the guest in. Over."

"Ten-four." Sutter said.

Keeley glanced away from Sutter for a moment to see Alec and Shane helping Judd to strip the wet clothes off his torso—but only for a moment. Because as Sutter stood there next to the pickup, bare from the waist up, she could not keep from staring at him. The man was ripped! His muscles were not only big but also incredibly defined. Add to that the fact that Sutter's body heat was apparently replenishing itself pretty well, being that his skin was a healthy color as opposed to the white-and-blue tint of Judd's. Keeley was nothing short of entirely dazzled!

"My dad will be here in just a few minutes," Sutter said as he strode to one of the snowmobiles parked nearby that had also been used to transport the De Carlo family out to the sledding area. "So don't worry. He'll get everyone back safely. I'm sorry I have to leave you, but your friend here is going to be in a bad way if we don't get him taken care of pretty quick."

Hopping onto the snowmobile, turning the key in the starter, and revving the engine a bit, Sutter glared at Judd. "You're gonna have to hold on, man. Think you can manage that?" he asked.

Judd didn't speak—only nodded.

Once Alec and Shane had helped Judd to sit on the snowmobile behind Sutter, Sutter said, "Hang on," and the snowmobile shot off down the road back toward the cabins, leaving Keeley standing there in wondering awe—over not only Sutter's heroics on Judd's behalf but also his incredible physique.

Everyone else stood with their mouths gaping open for a moment before Keeley's father finally turned to Ethan and said, "What part of *family* reunion did you not understand?"

CHAPTER FIVE

The "emotionally charged discussion" that transpired between Keeley's father and his sister Krystal once everyone had returned to the Snow Creek lodge had only added to everyone's stress. Oh, it wasn't too heated—but Keeley's dad had raised his voice, and Krystal had raised hers.

Joe told Krystal that Judd shouldn't have been there in the first place—that Krystal knew darn well Judd planned on trying to push Keeley into dating him, just as he always did, and that it was wrong for Krystal not to think of Keeley first, instead of pleasing Ethan and Judd. Krystal argued that she had no idea Judd was still fixated on Keeley, and if she had known, she would never have okayed his coming with them. Of course, everyone in the room knew that Krystal was just trying to cover her tracks.

But it didn't work. Joe De Carlo stood his ground and told Krystal she owed every family member an apology, and to his nephew Ethan he'd said, "And you're too old to be asking your mama if you can have a friend over."

Still, everything simmered down. Krystal apologized to everyone, and so did Ethan. As she was apologizing to Keeley, Krystal even offered to tell Judd he needed to leave. But, as always, Keeley had had a really difficult time saying what she really wanted to say—

which was, *Yes! Yes! Send him home! He's making my life miserable!* Instead, she just thanked her aunt for the apology, told her it was okay if Judd stayed (even though her father frowned at her when she did), and decided it was time to use the secret key Sutter had given her the night before.

After all, everyone in the De Carlo extended family scattered to the wind once the "discussion" was over. Sledding and tubing was fun, but it was physically taxing, and everybody was wiped out and ready for some rest before the family dinner scheduled that evening.

"I think you should take a little nap, Paiz," Keeley heard her mother tell her little sister as everyone began to return to their cabins.

"But, Mom," Paisley whined, "I'm not tired at all!"

"Well, I am," Cynthia said, "and so is your dad…and Keeley too. And you want to have fun at dinnertime and feel like playing games and things afterward, don't you?"

Frowning, Paisley mumbled, "Yeah."

"Then let's just rest a bit, okay?" Cynthia encouraged.

Head hanging in defeat, Paisley dragged her feet toward the exit.

"You coming, Keys?" Cynthia asked.

"Um…in a bit," Keeley answered. "I think I'd like to take a walk or something first."

Her mom winked, understanding that Keeley needed time away from everyone. Keeley had already decided she needed to tell her mom about the cabin; otherwise she'd worry if Keeley began to disappear here and there with no explanation.

I'll text you, she mouthed to her mom.

Cynthia nodded and, taking hold of Paisley's hand, headed out through the lodge's front door.

"I'm sorry about all this, sweetie," Keeley's dad said, coming to stand beside her. Putting a strong, comforting arm around her shoulders, he leaned down and whispered, "I swear I could beat the tar out of Krystal! I know you weren't happy about spending Christmas away from home and with the family at all anyway. And when I saw Ethan had brought Judd along…"

"It's okay, Dad," Keeley said. "Really."

Joe smiled down at his daughter. "No. It's not. But we're in it now, so let's just buckle up for the ride, I guess." He kissed the top of her head, adding, "I would've sent him packing when Krystal asked if she should if I were you though. That kid is too senseless to give up on pushing you…even after the circus he caused today."

"I know," Keeley sighed, realizing her dad was exactly right. No doubt Judd would recover from his near-death experience, show up at the family dinner that night, and act like nothing weird had happened at all.

"Hey, Dad?" Keeley said as her dad dropped his arm from around her shoulders and started toward the door.

"Yeah?" he asked, looking back to her.

Keeley looked around to make sure no one at all was within listening distance.

"I…um…Sutter gave me a key to a spare cabin," Keeley whispered, "in case Judd's determination started to drive me crazy. So…I'm going to go over there and take a nap or read or something, instead of going back with you guys. Is that okay?"

Joe smiled, nodding. "That Sutter sure is a perceptive guy, isn't he?" he asked in a whisper.

"It would seem so," Keeley agreed.

"Well, that sounds like a great idea to me," Joe said. "I think you could use a secret hideout, hmmm?"

"Yeah," Keeley sighed.

"We'll see you at dinner then, okay?"

"Of course! Thanks, Dad." Keeley tiptoed and placed a loving kiss on her father's scruffy face. "I'll see you in a bit."

"Okay," Joe said. Then he turned and headed out of the lodge himself.

Keeley inhaled a deep breath, exhaling a heavy sigh as she headed toward the back of the lodge. She figured it would be the best way to go unnoticed—exit through the lodge's back door and hurry to the cabin just a ways beyond. She was glad she'd decided to keep the key with her at all times, even pinning it to the inside of her jeans pocket when she left to go tubing that morning. Now she couldn't wait to get to the cabin, strip off her snowsuit, find the hot chocolate, and collapse in privacy.

As she reached the little cabin behind the lodge, Keeley again looked around to make sure no one was around to see where she was going. Then slipping the key into the doorknob, she turned it and pushed the door open when it unlocked.

The moment she stepped into the snug little cabin, Keeley felt better. Closing the door behind her and stepping through the small entryway, Keeley stood still for a moment, marveling at the perfect ambiance of the place. The main room was small, indeed, but also big enough for a loveseat and two comfortable-looking chairs all positioned to face the hearth and mantel on the far side of the room. Inviting, warm-looking rugs under the furniture added to the soft, warm sensation of the scene, and the lovely, white-lighted Christmas tree in the far left corner glowed softly, the lights reflecting in the quaint, vintage glass ornaments and long silver icicles. Naturally there were sprigs of holly, pine boughs, pinecones, and sprays of red berries here and there—even a beautiful white amaryllis in bloom on the mantel, surrounded by a dozen or so candles of various sizes and heights. A small kitchen to the right housed a rustic table-for-two and a reproduction white vintage woodstove, complete with a copper teakettle sitting on one burner plate. A small reproduction white refrigerator was also tucked neatly into one corner of the kitchen. All in all, the front of the little cabin felt and looked like something out of a storybook.

Keeley stripped off her snowsuit, hanging it on one of the hooks on the wall in the entryway before heading to the back of the cabin to check out the bedroom and bath. She giggled with delight as she stepped into the bedroom to see a sleigh-style bed laden with a red-and-black checked quilt and a plethora of comfortable-looking throw pillows to match. There was a pretty slider rocker and ottoman to the left of the bed and a door that opened to the bathroom to the right. The bathroom was small but still managed to house a claw-foot porcelain tub anyway.

Keeley couldn't imagine a more perfect hideout. The little cabin was perfect! And when she returned to the kitchen and opened a cupboard to find a myriad of different hot chocolate mixes and microwave popcorn available, Keeley filled the copper kettle with water from the kitchen faucet and set it to heating on the quaint little stove. Hot chocolate and popcorn—paired together, was there anything more soothing to eat and relish? Keeley thought not.

"I could live out my life here, I think," she sighed as she sat down on the loveseat in the front room and began looking through the small piles of books that were waiting on the coffee table. Choosing a beautifully illustrated book of Christmas poetry, Keeley texted her mom before settling in to read it.

"Hot chocolate, popcorn, Christmas poetry?" Keeley whispered to herself. "Seriously, I'm in heaven!"

♥

It was the soft knock on the front door that first roused Keeley from her warm, blissful slumber.

But it was Sutter's voice saying, "Hey, Keeley? Are you in there?" from the other side of the door that sent Keeley leaping off the cozy, warm loveseat and nearly sprinting for the door.

Smoothing her cockeyed ponytail and rubbing the sleep from her eyes, Keeley slapped on a groggy smile and opened the door.

Golly, he was gorgeous! The sight of Sutter standing there, wearing a barn coat and a black beanie, sent her heart fluttering and the butterflies that sprang up in her stomach to completely spazzing out!

"I'm sorry to bother you," Sutter began, "but I wanted to make sure you were okay—you know, after today...me losing my cool with your friend Judd and all."

"You mean losing your cool with Ethan's idiot friend, Judd, don't you?" she teased. "And if that's you losing your cool...wow! You're, like, the least angry guy I know."

"Well," Sutter sighed all the same, "it wasn't very professional, in the very least of it." He smiled, asking, "Would you mind if I came in for a minute?"

"Oh, I'd love it!" Keeley exclaimed, all too delighted to have Sutter step into the sweet little cabin with her.

"Thanks," Sutter said, stepping in and knocking the snow off his boots on the rubber rug at the entrance. He took off his beanie, stuffing it into one pocket of his barn coat. Removing his coat, he hung it next to Keeley's snowsuit. Keeley's smile broadened—for he wore only a tight-fitting, ecru, long-sleeved thermal undershirt beneath, and he looked delicious in it! The thermal underwear shirt fit him like a glove, accentuating every perfectly defined muscle in his arms, chest, and stomach. Keeley marveled at how much more attractive Sutter was standing there in thermal underwear, jeans, and boots than any other man dressed in any other fashion at all!

"I hope you don't think I'm a pig," Keeley said as he followed her into the cabin's cozy front room. "I made some hot chocolate and popcorn, read a little bit of a book, and dozed off, I guess."

Quickly she picked up the empty mug and microwave popcorn back off the coffee table and hurried it into the kitchen.

"I'm glad you were able to relax," Sutter called.

"Well, I have you to thank for it," Keeley said, quickly returning to the sitting room.

Sutter collapsed into one of the big, comfortable chairs, sighing, "Awwww." Smiling at her, he said, "What a day, huh?"

"You're not kidding," Keeley agreed. "How is Judd anyway? I'm assuming he's fine, but I didn't even think to ask…until now. Guess I was just so tired from playing in the snow."

"He's fine," Sutter assured her. "No worse for the wear, it would appear."

"If I know Judd—and I do, being that I've been avoiding him for, like, three years—he's probably acting like nothing even happened," Keeley offered.

"Pretty much…at least from what I've seen," Sutter said, nodding. "I don't think he gets how dangerous what he did was. He really could have died in the lake."

"But you saved him," Keeley pointed out.

"Naw," Sutter said, shaking his head. "I just drug him out of the lake. I should've known he'd be trying to impress you. I kind of thought he might try a stunt like he did—it's why I warned him about it. But…I guess he didn't believe me."

"He's just a smart-aleck city boy," Keeley offered. "He's always thought he knows more than anybody else in all the world. It's one of the things that drives me nuts about him. One of the many, many things."

"The guy is tenacious, I'll give him that," Sutter chuckled. "He'll pull out all the stops if he thinks it'll get your attention."

Keeley didn't want to talk about Judd anymore. She didn't want to talk about him at all! Even the thought of Judd made her teeth clench with irritation, and she wanted to enjoy whatever time she had isolated in the cute little cabin with Sutter.

"I hope you warmed up though," she said, attempting to somewhat change the subject of their conversation. "I can't imagine how cold that water was. Do you want some hot chocolate? Or some popcorn? I could make some for you."

"Sure," Sutter answered. "A guy can't go wrong with hot chocolate, popcorn, and the prettiest girl in the world making it for him."

Keeley blushed. "Oh, come on," she laughed. "You're not in trouble with me, so no need for flattery."

"I'm serious," Sutter contended. "In fact, I've been trying to get up the nerve to ask you for your number...but I'm not really good at facing rejection, so I've chickened out when I had the chance before."

"*You* chickened out about asking *me* for *my* number?" Keeley laughed as she headed into the kitchen to start the kettle to boiling again and pop some popcorn. "Ha! It took every thread of courage I could muster just to speak at all when I met you yesterday!"

Sutter puffed a laugh, saying, "Yeah, right." He sighed, raking a hand over his head and through his tousled hair. "But, seriously...how *are* you holding up?" he asked. "I mean, from what I can see, that Judd guy isn't going to give up too easily."

Keeley breathed a sigh of discouragement as she returned to the front room and plopped down on the loveseat. "I know," she admitted. "I wish he would just get the hint, you know?"

Sutter nodded, was quiet for a moment, and then ventured, "I'm assuming you've told him—probably more than once—that you're not really interested, right?"

Keeley shrugged. "Well, not directly," she admitted. "I mean, one would think that after my so obviously trying to avoid him—especially here—he'd get the hint, right? And I've told Ethan flat out a million times that Judd's not my type and that I'm just not interested at all. But he just keeps coming at me. I'm not sure what else I can do. I...I don't want to be mean and hurt his feelings."

"I understand," Sutter commiserated. "But guys like that...you just have tell them directly to their faces that you're not interested, or they don't ever give up. Actually, *girls* like that you just have speak plainly to, as well. It's not easy, but he's probably never going to get the hint if he hasn't by now. In truth, he probably *has* gotten the hint but just won't swallow it."

Keeley nodded. She knew Sutter was right—that she should just man up and tell Judd that she wasn't ever going to like him as anything other than a casual friend. But Keeley hated to hurt people's feelings, no matter the situation.

"But, hey," Sutter said then, "you're trying to relax, right? So no worrying about crazy-ass stalkers, okay?"

Keeley laughed. "Good idea!" Judd Sutherland was the last person on the face of the earth she wanted to think or talk about right then. Sutter Price, on the other hand—now that was a sexy subject she could really sink her teeth into.

"So let's talk about you instead," she suggested. "Where do you live? Just here on the premises?"

"Yes, ma'am," Sutter answered with a nod, "though not right near the rental cabins and lodge and stuff. I'm like you. I value my privacy—need it, actually. I own a cabin about a mile north."

"Wow, that must be awesome!" Keeley noted. "And you live here all the time? Like, year-round?"

Sutter nodded. "I do. Ever since I got back and decided to help my folks run the Snow Creek cabins. I mean, if I was hoping to impress a pretty girl sitting across the room from me, I might inadvertently mention that I even built the cabin I own and live in. Well, my dad and brothers helped me…a little."

He winked at her, smiling an alluring smile that Keeley figured could probably get him anything he wanted from anybody.

"Jinkies!" she breathed—and she was thoroughly impressed. Not only was Sutter gorgeous, manly, and capable, but he could also build his own cabin. "I admit to being dazzled!"

Sutter chuckled, saying, "Oh good! My plan worked."

Keeley giggled softly, delighted that Sutter apparently cared what she thought about him.

The kettle on the stove began to whistle, and she hopped back up, heading to the kitchen.

"What kind of popcorn do you want?" she called to him. "Whoever stocked this place has every kind imaginable."

She heard him chuckle, and then he said, "Kettlecorn, if there's that."

"Oh, there is that," she assured him, knowing full well he probably already knew it. She quickly put a bag of kettlecorn popcorn in the microwave, punched in the time indicated on the instructions, and set about making their hot chocolate.

Three and a half minutes later, she reentered the sitting room, placing two mugs of hot cocoa on two of the coasters on the coffee table and handing the bag of hot popcorn to Sutter. Yet something Sutter had said had struck her as curious as she'd been stirring his hot chocolate. And the more she'd thought about it, the more her intuition—her "scary intuition," as her brothers always called it— kicked in. Could the idea that had begun to linger in her mind be as insightful as her sudden thoughts often were where Sutter was concerned? As she often did, Keeley began to doubt herself. But she soldiered on anyway.

"You said that you've lived here ever since you 'got back' and decided to help your parents with Snow Creek," she began. "Did you 'get back' from military service perhaps?"

Sutter's eyebrows shot up in surprise. "What? Are you, like, some FBI profiler or something? I thought you were a ghostwriter," he said. "And yes, I did 'get back' from military service."

Keeley shook her head. "Nope. Not a profiler. Just a ghostwriter," she confirmed. "But sometimes I can just—I don't know—feel stuff about people."

Sutter shook his head with disbelief. He didn't seem angry or irritated—just astonished.

"Damn! I thought I hid it better than that," he mumbled as he smiled at her. "Did my Lego calluses give me away or what?"

Keeley giggled. "Your Lego calluses? What are you talking about?"

"Well, as I said, I did get back and decide I wanted to live out here and help with the cabins," he admitted. "But before I was ready to build my house, I had to work through…well, to be honest, I had a mild case of PTSD when I got home. I didn't even know it for a couple of months. But then my mom and dad noticed how jumpy and on edge I was all the time. They wanted me to go to the VA and see if there was someone there to help me out, you know. And even though I did, it was actually something my mom suggested that got me through it and taught me how to work it out. I just needed an outlet."

"Legos?" Keeley asked, not laughing. She knew how horrible any measure of PTSD could be—how debilitating. She also knew that activity, weight training, and exercise, as well as spending time in nature, were important therapy venues. Relaxation was also an important part of dealing with PTSD. And although most people employed deep-breathing and meditation techniques to help them relax, she could see how building and creating with Legos could have the same result.

Sutter nodded. "Yep. Legos," he affirmed.

Keeley waited—waited to see if Sutter wanted to change the subject or continue telling her about his experience. She knew it was important for veterans to make that choice.

"Mom reminded me that, when I was a kid, Legos were not just my thing for fun but my downtime thing too, you know?" he explained.

He'd chosen to tell her more about his experience, and Keeley was glad. She wanted to know everything about the incredible man sitting across from her—everything—the good and the bad.

"And as I hit the teen years," he continued, "you know…the angry adolescent boy who thinks he's invincible, thinks he knows everything, and can drive his parents nuts?"

Keeley nodded, offering, "The companion to the adolescent teen girl who never feels liked, thinks life will never get better, and bawls all the time?"

"Yeah," Sutter chuckled. "Anyway, my mom reminded me that, during those years, I used to go into my room, set up a TV tray, watch a movie, and build Legos for hours. I always came out of my room refreshed, less angry, and feeling better." He shrugged. "So when my folks figured out I was PTSDing, Mom went out and bought me this big Lego set. I mean big—4,016 pieces to be exact. The Star Wars Death Star one."

He paused for a moment, so Keeley inquired, "And did you build it? Did it work?"

Sutter nodded. "It did," he assured her. "I watched the entire Lord of the Rings movie trilogy." He winked and added, "The extended versions, mind you."

"Impressive," Keeley said, smiling.

"I watched them while I built the Death Star and then spent two more weeks building various and sundry Lego sets, as I immersed myself in rewatching my favorite movies. And after that…I got it. I had a lot of time to think, to process and everything, and although I was still jumpy occasionally for a bit…" He straightened in his chair, placed his hand over his heart, and said, "I'm Sutter Price, and I have PTSD…and Legos saved my life."

He smiled and winked at her, and she knew that even though he was being overly dramatic, he was also sincere.

"Wow," Keeley breathed in awe. "Your mom sounds like a great mom. She knew her son and knew what would help him."

"She did," Sutter agreed. "Of course, she won't take credit for anything. She says it was divine intervention that put the thought in her head. But either way, she opened her mouth and said it, right?"

"Faith can move mountains," Keeley offered.

"Or prompt a mother to tell her son to build Legos," he added.

Keeley nodded in agreement, thinking that Sutter's family must be as wonderful as he was. Her own mom was careful never to ignore a thought that entered her mind where her children were concerned either. And there had been many times growing up that

Keeley's brothers had been saved from disaster because their mom had listened to the same divine intervening voice that Sutter's had.

"So?" he asked then.

"So, what?" she giggled.

"So? I don't know how, but you guessed I had been in the military. Can you guess which branch of the military?" he playfully dared.

"Semper Fi, brotha," Keeley answered. "Oorah!"

Sutter immediately broke into laugher. "Girl! You *are* a profiler! How in the world did you guess? Seriously?"

Keeley shrugged. "I don't know," she answered. "You just seem like a boots-on-the-ground, combat arms, search-and-destroy kind of guy. You know…way capable of doing anything. Taking out insurgents or…or jumping off a mountain to save some dipshidiot's life."

Again Sutter's eyebrows arched in surprise. "Wow! I'm gonna have to watch myself with you, you little ghostwriting profiler girl."

"Naw," Keeley sighed, however. "I just got lucky this time." She looked at Sutter, studying him for a moment. He was so amazing! So humble. It was obvious he truly valued nature, his chosen field of work, and helping people have fun the way he'd helped her family at the sledding hill that morning.

Just then Keeley's phone chimed, indicating she was receiving a text. Discouraged that her isolated moments with Sutter had been interrupted, she picked up her phone and read the text message from her mom.

"Everything okay?" Sutter asked, sipping his hot chocolate before munching on a few kernels of kettlecorn.

"Yeah," Keeley answered. "Just my mom reminding me about the family dinner tonight." She exhaled heavy sigh and slumped back in the soft loveseat.

"Hey, it'll be fun," Sutter said. "I happen to know the food will be good."

Keeley looked at him to see him smiling at her with understanding—but also encouragement.

"Is that so?" she teased.

"Yep," he affirmed, nodding. "And when it's over—if you feel up to it, because I know you've had a long day—there's an almost full moon tonight, and it would be a great night to go owling," Sutter said.

Instantly Keeley's mood lightened. In that moment, she felt she could endure anything at all—even dinner with Judd present—if it meant she could go owling with Sutter afterward—if she could go anywhere at all with Sutter afterward.

"You mean, after this crazy day and spending so much time with my lunatic family, you'd still be willing to take me owling?" she asked him, afraid to believe what she'd heard him say was really what he'd said.

But he smiled, nodded, and assured, "Absolutely." He leaned forward, placing his hot chocolate mug back on the coaster on the coffee table. "Of course, I would need your cell number so I could, you know, call or text you to find out when you're finished with your family reunion commitments."

Keeley blushed with excitement. Sutter Price wanted her number! He was going to text or call! He was going to take her owling later that night! In that moment, Keeley knew pure gratification.

"Well, I would need yours too," she countered, matching his flirtatious gaze. "I mean, if you text or call, and I don't have your number in my phone…"

"208-867-5309," he blurted.

Keeley giggled, and Sutter watched as she put his number in her phone.

"Now text me, and I'll have your number," he suggested. "Text me something scandalous."

"Like what?" Keeley laughed.

Sutter shrugged. "I don't know—just something to hint to me that maybe you're almost as interested in getting to know me better as I am in getting to know you better."

Shaking her head, delighted with his subtle wooing techniques, Keeley sent him a text. She heard the buzzing of his cell vibrating in his back pocket and blushed when he retrieved it, smiling as he read her text.

"I think you're hot," he read the text aloud. "I can't wait to go owling with you, Super Stud Sutter Price."

His smile broadened, and he began to text, speaking out loud as he did. "*I think you're hot too, foxy lady, Keeley De Carlo.*"

"Foxy?" Keeley squealed with felicity as her phone chimed to indicate Sutter had sent the text. "Did you just call me *foxy?*"

"Yeah," he answered. "Foxy. It means hot, sexy, really pretty. You've never been called *foxy?* I mean, I know it's an old slang term, but still…I can't believe no one has ever called you that before."

"Oh, I know what it means," Keeley admitted, enchanted beyond measure at the fact he had called *her* foxy. "I'm just surprised you do…and that you would call me that."

"Well, you shouldn't be…on either account," Sutter said, rising from his chair.

As he stretched a little, Keeley's heart began aching at knowing he was getting ready to leave her. Still, he'd said they'd go owling later, after her family's dinner—and *that* was something to live for!

"I'll see you later then," he said, striding toward the front door.

"I sure hope so," Keeley responded as he pulled on his coat, fished his beanie out of the pocket, and pulled it onto his head.

Sutter winked. "Oh, you can bet your life on it, foxy."

"Okay," Keeley giggled as he opened the door, stepped over the threshold, and started walking away.

Keeley stood in the doorway, watching Sutter rather swagger toward the lodge. She loved the way his shoulders dipped and rose in opposition as he walked—the way his jeans fit over his long, muscular legs and butt.

"Mmmm mmm, Mr. Price! Boom-boom-foxy, indeed!" she whispered to herself. Then she giggled, thinking how fun it would be to tell Paisley that Sutter Price had called Keeley *foxy*—someday anyway.

CHAPTER SIX

Keeley smiled as she returned Sutter's text. He was swinging by to pick her up and was almost to the Cozy Cabin.

"Now...what's this you're doing again, Keys?" Joe De Carlo asked.

"We're going owling, Dad," Keeley answered.

"Owling, hmm? Is that what they're calling it these days?" Joe inquired, winking at Keeley with a glint of mischief in his eyes.

Keeley sighed and rolled her eyes. "Don't be a dork, Dad," she giggled. Yet in truth, her father's inference that she and Sutter were using "owling" as an excuse to make out caused goose bumps to race over her arms and legs. Oh, she knew Sutter wouldn't kiss her—not after knowing her only a day and half. But a girl could daydream, couldn't she?

Keeley's phone tinged again, indicating another text.

"What's Sutter suggesting now? Nesting?" Joe teased. "Seems like a logical activity after owling."

"Joe," Cynthia scolded—although she was smiling too.

"No," Keeley answered. "He's just telling me to make sure I dress very warmly. He says it's already only fifteen degrees outside and will be colder by the time we get to the place he has in mind."

"Hmm," Joe hummed. "If it were me and I was taking your mother 'owling'"—Joe made quotation marks with his fingers—"I'd be sure she underdressed for the cold weather instead of dressing extra warm."

"Why?" Keeley and her mother chimed in unison.

"So that *I* could provide the extra warmth for her," Joe answered. He shimmied his eyebrows and mumbled, "If you know what I mean?"

"Dad! I hardly know the guy!" Keeley gasped—though the idea of Sutter providing her with extra warmth by way of his muscular arms around her caused more goose bumps to erupt over her various appendages.

"I'm just saying," Joe added, shaking his head. "I could teach that kid a thing or two about owling."

There was a soft knock on the front door of the cabin then, and Keeley hurried to answer it.

She opened the door to find Sutter looking as delicious as ever! He was wearing a much heavier coat, a black scarf, and his black beanie.

"Hi," he greeted with a smile.

"Hi," Keeley offered in return. She was sure she was grinning like a psychopath, but she couldn't help it! Sutter was just so...so—

"Are you sure you're still up for this?" Sutter asked. "It's freaking cold out tonight."

"Oh, I'm sure," Keeley guaranteed. She didn't care if she got frostbite or froze to death even. She knew being with Sutter would be worth any discomfort from the cold. And anyway, as long as she was with him, her heart would stay warm no matter what.

"Good evening, Sutter," Joe said as he approached the front door, as well. "I hear you two are going 'owling,'" he said, again gesturing quotation marks with his fingers.

"Yep," Sutter affirmed. "It's really cool to be out there and see the big ones fly over…or sit studying you from a perch in a tree. They don't always show up though, so I'm hoping we're lucky tonight."

"Well, if they don't show, I'm sure you'll think of something to do out there in the dark," Joe teased, winking dramatically.

"Joe De Carlo! You knock that off!" Cynthia scolded from her place on a big chair next to the fire. "Just ignore him, Sutter. He's had too much sugar today."

"Yes, ma'am," Sutter chuckled. Then offering a gloved hand to Keeley, he said, "Well, if you're ready."

"Very ready," Keeley admitted.

But as she reached out to take his hand, Sutter said, "Oh! Wait! I almost forgot."

Keeley watched as he rummaged around in his coat pocket, producing another black beanie.

Offering it to her, he said, "You should wear this one instead." Unfolding it, he held it out to her. "See? It's one of my tactical hoods. See how it covers everything but your eyes? It's super warm. You'll be amazed at how much it helps."

"Wow…I've never worn tactical gear before," Keeley said as she accepted the hood. Stripping off her ivory crocheted beanie, she pulled the black hood over her head and face, smoothing it around her neck. "Holy smokes! You weren't kidding. It's way warmer!"

"Oh good," Joe said. "We certainly wouldn't want you catching a cold while you're out 'owling' tonight, now would we."

"Joe…you've beat the joke into the ground, okay? Lay off," Cynthia laughed.

Winking at Keeley, Joe said, "But really…you two have fun." He nodded to Sutter, adding, "And we won't wait up, Keys. Being with the family all day wore us out."

"Okay, Dad," Keeley said.

Sutter offered his hand again, and this time Keeley took it.

"Good night, Mr. De Carlo," Sutter said, nodding to her father. Then looking to where her mother sat, he said, "Good night, Mrs. De Carlo. Sleep well."

"Thank you, Sutter," Cynthia called.

When Keeley stepped out onto the porch, Sutter didn't let go of her hand the way she'd supposed he would. Instead, he held her hand the entire time they were walking to his truck. Oh sure, it wasn't as wonderful as it would have been had they not both been wearing gloves. But it was romantic all the same and caused Keeley's heart to leap with excitement.

Sutter opened the passenger door of the big white Dodge pickup and closed it for Keeley once she had stepped up and settled in the seat.

Pulling at his beanie, revealing it was a tactical hood like the one he'd given Keeley, Sutter adjusted it so that the opening for his eyes was tucked under his chin, revealing his entire face instead of just his eyes. He hurried around the front of the pickup, slid into the driver's seat, closed his door, and shifted into drive. The pickup had been running when they'd reached it, and Keeley was glad, for the heat coming from the front console was warming.

"We're going out to this little patch of woods right behind my place," Sutter explained as he drove. "There's a great horned owl that lives there. I hear him every night, and I've seen him any time I've tried to. So I think he's our best bet." Sutter looked at Keeley and winked, adding, "Let's hope he doesn't turn bashful on us when he sees how pretty you are, all decked out in your red coat and tactical hood."

Keeley giggled and stretched the opening of the tactical hood so that it was tucked under her chin, revealing her entire face the way Sutter did his.

"Well, I've never felt sexier than I do right now, wearing this," Keeley laughed. "Although it does hide my hair, so Mr. Great Horned Owl might actually mistake me for a dude."

But Sutter shook his head. "Nobody could ever mistake you for anything but a fine, foxy-thang woman. Believe me," he assured her.

Keeley blushed, perfectly titillated by his complimentary flirting.

"So…how does this work?" she asked. "Do we just waltz out to the woods and wait?"

Sutter shrugged broad shoulders, answering, "Kind of. We walk out into the woods, as quiet as we can—no talking and stuff. I'll do a couple of owl calls here and there…and then, hopefully, he'll show up."

"It's that easy?" Keeley asked.

"Yes and no," Sutter began. "It's that easy to try and get him to show up—walking out there in silence, calling him. But it's the 'will he show up or not' part that's sometimes hard. I'm not going to lie; it can be really disappointing when he doesn't come out. But that's why I always determine to just enjoy the outing, the moonlight, stars, falling frost, moon—stuff like that. If you decide you're going to like it whether or not an owl shows up, then it's always worth your time."

"Well, I'm determined this will be a magical night to remember," Keeley sighed with anticipation of the beautiful adventure before her.

Sutter smiled—because he hoped it would be a magical night to remember too. Keeley De Carlo was seeping into him somehow. It may have been more correct to say she had absorbed him—or he had absorbed her. Whatever the words were to describe what he was feeling, how attracted to her he was, Sutter didn't have them. What he was able to tell himself was that he'd never felt so drawn to any woman before—not ever.

Sutter had quit counting how many times the words "soul mate" or "my other half" had dominated his thoughts whenever he was in Keeley's company. He knew anybody would think he was nuts if he confessed that she was "the one" for him, and he knew it. But that didn't keep him from knowing it was true. Oh, he'd keep it to himself—at least for now—but he knew that what his mind, heart, and body were telling him was true. Keeley was meant for him. The trick was trying to keep his hands off her long enough, and keeping the secret to himself long enough, for her to realize it.

Still, as he parked the pickup in his driveway—as he went around to her side of it, opened her door, and helped her step down—Sutter wondered how he was going to resist blurting out to her that he knew they were predestined for one another.

"It's beautiful out here!" Keeley quietly exclaimed as she stood studying Sutter's cabin. Smiling, she turned to him and said, "I can totally see why you chose to build here. The wooded area stretching out behind, the view of the distant mountains out your front window—I'm mean, wow!"

Sutter was pleased that she liked the place. It was further testament of her like-mindedness to him.

"And you've got white lights on the outside," she noted aloud. She leaned over, peeking in through the cabin's front window. "And a tree inside." She turned to him, her smile broadening with approval. "I like a man who has his own Christmas tree."

"Well, I like a woman who likes a man who has his own Christmas tree," he chuckled. "I'll take you for a tour inside when we're finished trying to coax that big boy out to greet us tonight if you like."

"I would love it!" she assured him, her eyes catching the moonlight and seeming to hold it as they glistened.

"Okay, then…let's go," Sutter said. "Now stick close to me, and remember no talking. It'll spook him."

"Will our walking in the snow scare him off, do you think?" Keeley asked.

"Not if we don't talk," he answered.

"But it's the sticking close to me part that's the most important, okay?" Sutter said, winking at her.

Keeley was awash in enchantment. Certainly, had any other guy she'd known only a day tried to flirt with her the way Sutter was doing, she'd have thought he was a jerk. But when Sutter did it, something was entirely different. It was almost as if she'd known him her whole life—expected him to be exactly as flirtatious as he was being. It was as if she'd always known him, and even though she knew she hadn't—that she'd only known him little more than thirty-six hours—she couldn't shrug off what her heart was telling her—that any moment she'd go from liking him more than any other man she'd ever known in all her life to being in love with him.

"Okay," she said, stepping closer to him.

An approving smile spread across his handsome face, and he nodded as he put one gloved index finger to his lips to let her know the time had come for no talking. Then taking her hand, he began to lead her around the side of his cabin toward the woods.

Just as Keeley was wondering how on earth they would see where they were going once they got into the trees and lost some of the moonlight, Sutter reached into his coat pocket and winked at her in letting her know he had read her thoughts. She smiled and nodded as he returned the flashlight to his pocket and led her into the woods.

There was no wind in the woods—not even a breeze—and Keeley was glad. The quiet was wonderful! The only sound was that of their footsteps—the soft crunch of the snow beneath their boots. At least, that was the only sound Keeley noticed at first. But as she continued to walk hand in hand with Sutter—as they trod further into the woods—all was so quiet and still that Keeley could hear the frost falling through the trees—actually hear the frost falling! In all her life she had never heard frost. In fact, until that moment, she hadn't imagined that falling frost even made a sound—but it did. Undoubtedly, it was almost imperceptible, but it was there—stilled, whist, a hushed chime, like a fairy's footstep.

Every pine shimmered as the moonlight kissed the frost, sending tiny, brief blinks of iridescent light skipping along their branches. It was truly a magical scene, something taken from a storybook, and Keeley half expected to glance over to Sutter and see him wearing knight's armor and carrying a broadsword, rather than wearing his coat and caching a flashlight in his pocket. The ethereal sensation of those minutes was that otherworldly to Keeley.

She was surprised when Sutter stopped so soon after they had breached the tree line. Letting go of her hand (which immediately felt colder for the loss of his touch—even for his glove), Sutter cupped his hands at his mouth and quietly called, "Whoo whoo…whooooo…whooooo. Whoo whoo…whoooo…whooo."

Beneath her tactical hood, Keeley's mouth gaped open a moment in astonished awe. Sutter's call sounded exactly like that of a great horned owl—exactly!

They stood very still together for a time. Then, shrugging at Keeley as he looked at her, he again took hold of her hand and led her further into the trees.

It was cold—very cold—and Keeley was grateful Sutter had thought to bring her the warmer headgear. Although her hands, feet, and legs were protected and somewhat warm, she could sense that the heat the hood kept her from losing through the top of her head was keeping the rest of her body warmer than it otherwise would have been.

They walked a ways—Keeley had no idea how far—until, quite unexpectedly to her, they stepped into a clearing. Keeley thought that it was probably a small meadow—green and lush in spring and summer, white and sparkling with frost in winter. Whatever the case, it was beautifully lit by the moonlight. Keeley wondered why Sutter was stopping there, on the edge of an open space. Surely any owl would steer clear of such a vulnerable spot.

"Whoo whoo…whooooo…whoooo. Whoo whoo…whoooo… whooo," Sutter called again.

Keeley almost gasped, barely remembering how important silence was, when from somewhere near came the call of the great horned owl in response. "Whoo whoo…whoooo….whooo."

Sutter grinned, looked to Keeley, and shimmied his eyebrows with pride and gratification.

"Whoo whoo…whoooo…whooo," he called once more.

"Whoo whoo…whooo…whooo," the owl called back.

This time, however, Sutter was expecting the echoing answer. Reaching into his pocket, he removed the flashlight, clicked it on, and shone it up into a tree to the right of the place they stood.

Keeley was surprised to find her eyes moistened with tears of not only being pleased that they had found the owl but also admiration for the beautiful creature in itself. There, perched on a bare birch branch, was the king who ruled the woods behind Sutter's house. The owl was much larger than Keeley had expected him to be. He looked to be about two feet in height with amber eyes that spoke of a day hunter—a brave, courageous hunter.

The owl sat studying Sutter and Keeley for what seemed several minutes. And then, all at once, it stretched its wings to a span Keeley thought must've been that of at least her own height, swooped down across the frosty meadow and up toward the silver-white moon, and disappeared over the treetops.

"Whoo whoo…whoooo…whoooo," she heard it call in the distance.

"Wow," Keeley breathed, awestruck by the experience.

She turned and looked to Sutter, smiling at him but not speaking. He didn't speak either, for it felt as if voices would somehow blemish the quiet moment—the beautiful, falling frost, owling moment.

After a time, however, Sutter tugged at the bottom of the opening of his tactical hood. Pulling it down and tucking it under his chin, he said at last, "Merry Christmas to you, Keeley De Carlo."

Keeley pulled at her hood, tucking it under her chin as well. "You have no idea," she said in a whisper.

"Don't I?" Sutter breathed as he unexpectedly stripped off his gloves, tossing them to the snowy ground as he reached out, taking Keeley's face between his warm, strong hands.

"No, you don't," Keeley respired the moment before he kissed her.

Her lips were softer than any velvet, sweeter than any fruit or candy, and as Sutter kissed Keeley gently several times in succession—as he waited for an indication from her that she liked him as much as he liked her—he wondered how he'd ever manage to make himself let her go again.

"Y-you don't really know me very well," she whispered when he paused in kissing her again. "I mean, you've only known me a day…maybe a little more. You don't even know me."

"Yes, I do," Sutter said, however, gathering her into his arms when he felt her fist the front of his coat in her hands and pull him closer to her.

It was her *Yes!*—her *Kiss me!* gesture—the way she melted against him—wrapped her arms around his shoulders. And he wasn't about to miss the opportunity to prove to her that he really did know her.

As Sutter's mouth pressed to hers, as Keeley returned his kiss—their lips blending in such a perfect cadency and shared bliss that she thought she might take flight from the rapturous sensation of it—Keeley's thoughts scattered with the falling frost. The only thing in her mind was Sutter—of how perfectly they kissed together, as if they had been kissing for years. Sutter—he was so handsome, so kind, compassionate, and yet strong and capable.

His kisses deepened, and Keeley met their depth unafraid, unashamed, and boldly. Something was happening to her—and, she sensed, to him too. In those minutes, as her feet tried to remind her they were cold—as she heard the great horned owl calling in the distance—Keeley De Carlo changed. As Sutter continued to kiss her—sometimes tenderly, sometimes with such intense intimacy Keeley thought she might faint with ecstasy—Keeley De Carlo knew her life had turned on a dime. With each moist, hot kiss, Sutter Price (perhaps unknowingly) laid claim to her heart—and to the rest of her life.

CHAPTER SEVEN

Sutter's cabin was warm and inviting—comfortable, perfectly decorated (by his mother, he had explained), and homey. The furniture in the cozy den comprised strong, masculine pieces—heavy wood framing with comfortable, firm cushions and throw pillows—and was arranged so that the large stone fireplace was the focal point of the room. An old steamer trunk served as a coffee table in the midst of the sitting area, and the masculine light fixtures, such as the chandelier crafted from deer antlers, gave the room an ambiance of relaxation as well as security in lingering. Sutter had started a fire the moment they had returned from owling—for even for the heated kisses they'd shared in the woods, they were both chilled to the bone.

Sutter had gone to the kitchen to pop some popcorn and put a kettle on the stove so that they could have hot chocolate, as well. And as Keeley sat in the cozy, comfortable room, studying every detail, her attention rested for a while on the beautiful mantel above the hearth. Constructed from sturdy logs instead of a simple wood shelf or slab, she marveled how perfectly it complemented the room. There was a taxidermied moose head hanging above the mantel as the center point, its massive antlers adorned with gold and red glass ornaments attached to varying lengths of thin, gold ribbon that hung from its handsome rack, adding a festive flavor to the room. Pine boughs lined the surface of the mantel, and ivory candles of varying heights and widths were placed here and there throughout it.

Next year we'll have to add some holly or red berries to give the mantel a little more color, Keeley thought to herself.

Instantly, she silently scolded herself, however, for such a ridiculous thought popping into her head. Not that holly or red berries wouldn't add to the mantel decor—they would. But thinking she would be there the next Christmas—that she'd thought "we"—as if a miracle would take place and she'd find herself married to Sutter before next Christmas.

She wondered if Sutter's incredible, delicious, almost supernaturally perfect kiss had somehow killed a significant amount of her brain cells. What other reason could there be for her having such ridiculous fantasies?

"Here we go," Sutter said, returning from the kitchen then. "I've got the water on the stove to boil, but let's not wait for that to eat the popcorn. I'm starving for some reason."

Sitting down on the sofa next to her and across from the fireplace, Sutter exhaled a heavy sigh of contentment, propped his shoeless, red-socked feet up on the steamer trunk coffee table, and set the large bowl of popcorn on the far side of Keeley, snagging a handful of double-buttered for himself before leaning back and looking at the fire.

"I love fire," he said.

"Me too," Keeley agreed—because it was true, after all. To Keeley there was nothing more relaxing than sitting before a fire and just watching the wood burn, the embers glimmer and glow, and listening to the soothing pops and cracks as it burned.

"No, I'm serious," Sutter offered, looking to her and grinning. "I love fire. I love it so much that sometimes I'll just sit at the table or outside near the fire pit and strike matches just to watch them burn."

Keeley giggled. "So you're a pyromaniac?"

His smile broadened, and he popped a kernel of popped corn into his mouth. "Naw. I don't have the urge to burn things down— just watch the fire, smell the wood smoke, stuff like that."

"Oh, good," Keeley sighed with dramatics. "But seriously, I like fire too. I could sit here all night and just watch that fire burn."

"Well, you're welcome to do it," Sutter said.

"Really?" she asked, quirking an eyebrow. "You'd let me stay here all night just watching your fire?"

"Of course," Sutter assured her. "I mean, baby…it's cold outside, you know?"

Keeley laughed, delighted by his quoting one of her favorite Christmas songs.

"That's one of my favorite songs…no matter what anyone says," she confessed.

Sutter's handsome brows puckered. "What do you mean? Who says what about that song? I grew up listening to my parents sing it here and there throughout the whole year…but especially at Christmas."

"Haven't you heard?' Keeley asked. "There's a faction that are claiming that song is filthy! That it's about a guy trying to force a girl into…into…you know…going to bed with him."

"What?" Sutter exclaimed, his frown deepening with disgust. "Who thought that up?"

Keeley shrugged. "I don't know—somebody with a dirty mind that can take anything and make it seem sexual."

"Well, that really chaps my ass," Sutter growled as he glared into the fire. Looking to Keeley, he apologized, "Sorry. But it does."

"Mine too," Keeley agreed. "When someone first told me I was a pervert for liking that song, I did a lot of research on it. It's a call-and-response song, as they term it…written by Frank Loesser in 1944. He and his wife performed it at parties and stuff, and it became such a huge hit that people would have parties revolving around the fact that Frank and Lynn would sing the duet there. Everyone gets all uptight about the line, 'What's in this drink?' because nowadays date rape drugs are put in drinks, you know? But back then, 'What's in this drink?' was a way of people blaming their behavior on something besides themselves, you know? And girls never were supposed to stay late or overnight with their boyfriends or fiancé, so even though the girl *wants* to stay with him, she had to make up an excuse—you know, so that it doesn't seem like it was her idea but only that she drank too much…you know, if people found out she stayed and stuff."

"Yeah, I never thought it was about a guy forcing a girl to stay or drugging her or something like that," Sutter commented. "People are so willing to believe the worst of everything, you know?"

"I do," Keeley affirmed. "But I'm reading this book right now that's helping me to deal with stuff like that a little better."

"A self-help book? What's it called?" he asked.

"Well, it's not really a self-help book per se," Keeley began. "It's more about understanding yourself so that you can deal with other people better. It's called *The Comprehensive INFP Survival Guide*."

Sutter sat up straight in his seat, his mesmerizing eyes widening with surprise. Keeley thought it was because the kettle in the kitchen had begun to whistle.

But when he said, "You're an INFP? I'm an ISFJ!" she realized it wasn't the kettle that had surprised him but Keeley's referencing her personality type.

"Y-you're familiar with the Myers-Briggs Foundation? The 16 Personality Type stuff?" Keeley asked. She was astonished! The only other people she'd ever known who had taken the personality type tests were her parents.

"Yes, ma'am," Sutter answered emphatically. "A guy I served with told me about it." He shrugged. "And even though I was a scoffer at first, I'm a believer now. That place is spot on…at least with me."

"Me too!" Keeley chirped. She was so happy—so excited to know that Sutter Price would understand something that no one other than her family had ever understood about her.

"Wow," Sutter said, nodding and smiling—obviously very pleased. He stood up and headed toward the kitchen. "Let me get our hot chocolate real quick, and then we can share notes, okay?"

"Okay," Keeley answered as her heart began to swell in her chest.

She was an INFP—a diplomatic mediator who was guided by her principles instead of logic. INFPs valued beauty, virtue, honor, and morality. Although people thought Keeley was shy, bashful, and always calm, the truth was Keeley's inward passion and desire to find the good in everything made her strong. Oh, sure, she was emotional—but emotion wasn't fragility. Still, most people thought that it was. Keeley figured Sutter—having taken the test and obviously done research on his own personality type, ISFJ—may well have run across information on INFPs—that he might "get" her, whereas so many other people (Judd popped into her mind) rarely did.

She could hear Sutter clattering around in the kitchen. No doubt he was impatient to make their hot chocolate and get back to talking with her.

"ISFJ. The Defender," she said, smiling. Keeley had read a lot on every personality type, and her favorite to read about, other than her own, was the ISFJ. Most INFPs chose to be poets, writers, and actors, whereas ISFJs were the personality type who landed in careers such as the military, law enforcement, medicine, firefighters, forest rangers, and social workers. The more Keeley thought about it, the more she realized that, even if Sutter hadn't told her he was an ISFJ, she would've put him in that very category based simply on what she had witnessed about him during the short time they'd spent together. She thought of his kindness to Paisley—his true caring for a little girl's feelings. She thought about the calm manner in which he warned Judd about the danger of the frozen lake—and about the way Sutter then, without hesitation, slid to Judd's rescue. Even the fact that he worked in the family business of running the Snow Creek cabins was evidentiary of his valuing family and tradition above all else.

"He really is a dream come true," Keeley sighed, smiling.

"What's that?" Sutter said, returning at that moment with two mugs of steaming hot chocolate.

"ISFJ, huh?" Keeley said, smiling at him as he set the mugs on two coasters on the steamer trunk. "I should've known."

"You being an INFP is what I should have known," he chuckled. "You're a ghostwriter, for crying out loud! And you like poetry." He sat down next to her on the sofa, reaching across her lap and procuring another handful of popped corn. "No wonder you can't tell that Judd guy to get lost. You INFPs are the most empathetic people around."

"And you…military veteran, cabin-building, family business guy," Keeley laughed. "You're a *total* ISFJ! *I* should've known."

"It's crazy, right?" Sutter said, eating his popcorn. "You're an I-N-freakin'-F-P. I love it!"

I love you, Keeley thought to herself as she ate a few kernels of popcorn too.

"Well, I'm glad you approve of my personality type," she teased.

"Oh, believe me, I do," he assured her with a wink. He finished the popcorn in his hand and then reached out and picked up one of the mugs of hot chocolate. "In fact," he began. He took a sip of the hot chocolate, frowning and setting it back down. "It's still too hot, sorry. But the truth is, I'm so excited about your being an INFP that I feel the need to kiss you again."

"I'm glad," Keeley said as Sutter put an arm around her shoulders, cradling her chin in his free hand. "Because I feel the need to be kissed by you again."

Sutter grinned, his green-blue eyes simmering with desire in the flicker of the firelight.

Their first kiss—their owling kiss—had been magnificent! Unexpected and more marvelous than anything Keeley had ever known, the kisses she and Sutter had shared while in the woods were all-consuming and nearly overwhelming with their emotional and physical power! Yet as they sat on the sofa in Sutter's warm, cozy, beautiful home, warmed by the fire and their desire, Keeley found she was much more relaxed—much more comfortable—and she melted against him, feeling at ease, safe, and enraptured.

As he kissed her, Sutter skillfully caressed her cheek and trailed his fingers over her neck, sending goose bumps racing over every inch of her flesh. His mouth was hot—tasted of peppermint hot cocoa and buttered popcorn. And his face—the stubble of a few days' whisker growth prickling at the tender flesh around Keeley's mouth—was also warm, smelling faintly of wood smoke, leather, and pine. Sutter smelled so good, in fact—kissed with such skill and magnificence—that Keeley's heart leapt with such force, she could no longer contain her desire to hold onto him tighter—kiss him more intensely. Therefore, breaking from him just long enough to pull her knees under her on the sofa so as to kneel next to him, she reached out, taking his face in her hands and applying a kiss to his mouth so vigorous and thirsting that Sutter chuckled in his throat with approval before wrapping his arms around her and pulling her down to sit on his lap as he returned her intrepid kiss with an even stronger, dauntless prowess.

After a long time—Keeley could not have told anyone exactly how long if someone had asked—Sutter broke the seal of their exchange of affection, held her face in his hands a moment while gazing into her eyes, and began, "Do you know what I just realized?"

Keeley blushed—bashful at the way his attention lingered on her mouth. "No. What?" she asked in a breathy whisper.

"We're conspiring," he said, smiling at her.

"What? What do you mean, we're conspiring?" she inquired—too intoxicated by everything about him to think clearly.

"You know...like in the song," he explained. "*Later on...we'll conspire*," he sang in a perfect, and very seductive, singing voice.

Keeley smiled, nodded toward the fireplace, and quietly sang, "*As we dream...by the fire.*"

"*To face unafraid*," Sutter mumbled-sang against her mouth, "*the plans that we've made...*" He pressed a long, lingering kiss to her lips. "*Walking in a...*"

"*Winter wonderland*," Keeley joined him in breathing the last words of the line to the song a moment before he gathered her in his arms, claiming her mouth again in a powerful, impassioned kiss.

If she was sure of anything, it was that her toes were no longer cold. Instead they were warm and toasty and curling in her socks for the sake of the euphoria she was bathing in as Sutter kissed her and she kissed him.

"Wanna make plans with me, Keeley De Carlo?" Sutter asked, his voice low and brimming with desire.

"What kind of plans?" Keeley asked. She still couldn't think rationally. In fact, she was so inebriated by his skillful ability to woo her that she really did wonder if something was in the hot chocolate—something the like of what the woman's part in "Baby, It's Cold Outside" implied.

Sutter shrugged. "I don't know yet," he answered. "Just…plans."

"Well, then…sure," Keeley agreed without even knowing what she was agreeing to.

Taking her face between his warm, strong hands, Sutter smiled at her for a long time. "We better get up and do something else for a while, before I do something I shouldn't," he suggested.

"Like what?" Keeley asked, recognizing the provocative tone in her own voice—even though she hadn't consciously meant to put it there.

Sutter laughed, "Ooo, girl! You are dangerous!"

"But really…what do you want to do?" Keeley asked, blushing with mild humiliation in realizing what he thought she'd implied.

Grinning with mischief, and in an alluring voice that made Keeley's toes tingle, he said, "You wanna see my Legos?"

"What?" Keeley gasp-laughed.

"Do you wanna see my Legos?" Sutter repeated. "Meaning my real Legos…in one of the bedrooms of the house. I know it might seem stupid to some people, but I really do have a Lego room."

"Oh! Do I wanna see your *Legos*," Keeley giggled. "For a minute I thought you were being metaphorical and…"

Sutter laughed, admitting, "That's what I wanted you to think."

"You're naughty!" Keeley exclaimed, teasingly slapping him on one solid shoulder.

"But really…I'm pretty proud of my Lego room," he clarified. "Wanna come see it?"

"I certainly do," Keeley assured him.

"Then come on," Sutter said, rising from the couch and offering his hand to her. Keeley took hold of his hand, standing up herself—overjoyed when he held onto it as he led her toward the back of the house. "Maybe my sick Lego skills can win you over, if my kissing skills didn't."

"Oh, if your Lego skills are as masterful as your kissing skills…I'm in trouble," Keeley giggled.

How could it be? she wondered as she followed Sutter farther into his house. How could it be that what had started out as something akin to a prison sentence to her—a family reunion away from home at Christmastime—had ended up being the most marvelous, life-changing experience of her life?

CHAPTER EIGHT

"You look like you're still tired, Keys," Paisley noted aloud.

Taking a bite of the slice of poppy seed bread his wife was serving as part of their Christmas Eve morning breakfast, Joe De Carlo added, "That's what happens when you don't get to bed until almost five a.m."

Keeley glanced up from her own breakfast plate to see her father staring at her as her mother giggled, "Joe, don't talk with your mouth full in front of the girls."

"Is five a.m. very late to go to bed?" Paisley asked.

"Very, *very* late," her mother answered. "But now that you're finished with your breakfast, why don't you run on in and get dressed for the day? We've got lots of fun planned, and we want to be ready on time."

"Okay, Mom," Paisley agreed, hopping down off her chair. "And can I still wear my candy cane dress tonight to Christmas Eve dinner?"

"Of course," Cynthia assured her daughter.

"It's my favorite one because Daddy bought it for me special for this trip," Paisley added as she sprinted off toward the bedroom she and Keeley shared in the Cozy Cottage.

As soon as Paisley was out of earshot, Cynthia leaned over the table, whispering to Keeley, "Did you swap out the you-know-what for the you-know-what?"

"I did," Keeley quietly assured her mother.

"What's a you-know-what and a you-know-what?" Joe asked.

"Shhh!" Keeley and her mother simultaneously shushed him.

"You know, Joe—the calendar that Keeley was going to give to Paisley...that Paisley asked Santa for. Keeley's giving the calendar to Santa to give to Paiz, and Santa gave Keeley the mermaid tail blanket he was going to give to Paiz. They're swapping, remember?" Cynthia explained.

"Oh yeah, now I do," Joe mumbled. "Although, if you ask me, there's something wrong with a six-year-old wanting a Johnny Depp calendar in the first place."

Keeley and her mother exchanged glances, shaking their heads in unison.

"It's not a Johnny Depp calendar, Joe," Cynthia said. "It's a Jack Sparrow calendar."

"And the difference is...what? Eyeliner?" Joe teased. "I think that disturbs me even more."

"Oh, Dad," Keeley giggled. "You're just not a girl."

"That's true," Joe admitted. Then putting one elbow on the table and leaning closer to Keeley, he said, "But I *am* a man. And a dad too. Furthermore, I wouldn't be a good dad if I didn't ask you what you were doing out until five a.m. with a man you've known two and half days."

Keeley smiled and nodded. "No...you wouldn't," she agreed. "But I promise you, Dad, we were just talking and stuff."

"It's the 'and stuff' that worries me," Joe said—though he winked at Keeley with a mischievous glint in his eyes all the same.

"It's serious, isn't it, Keys?" Cynthia inquired. In truth, it sounded more like a statement—as if her mother were only asking to open up a venue for Keeley to confess to her father that it was serious. It was one of the things she admired and loved about her mom—her ability to play the mediator without anyone really knowing that she was doing it.

"I...I think it will be," Keeley admitted. She picked up her fork and began poking at the leftover scrambled egg bits on her plate.

"How serious is it?" Joe asked then.

"Well, Dad...like you said, we've only been here a little while," Keeley stammered. "And I...I can't really say. I mean, if I were to tell you what I'm really thinking, you'd think I was crazy and—"

"I told you, Joe," Cynthia unexpectedly interjected. "I told you the moment we saw that boy that he was the one for our Keeley. You owe me a hundred bucks! I told you!"

"What?" Keeley exclaimed, astonished.

"Yeah, yeah, yeah," Joe moaned. "But the jury is still out. It's only been a couple of days."

"You proposed to me on our first date," Cynthia reminded her husband. "We stayed out all night New Year's Eve, until seven a.m. New Year's Day. And by the time you brought me home that morning, we both knew we were meant for one another. So why should you doubt my mother's intuition where our children are concerned, hmmm?"

Joe shrugged. "Well, I'm still not paying you the hundred 'til I see a ring on that finger," he said, gesturing toward Keeley's left ring finger.

For her part of it, Keeley sat looking back and forth between her parents, her mouth gaping open in utter stupefaction. What were her parents saying? That they weren't surprised that Keeley was already head-over-heels in love with Sutter? And how could her mother possibly have known the moment she met Sutter that he would be the one to claim Keeley's heart? Yet as the conversation between her parents had a chance to really soak into her brain, she realized that she wasn't surprised at all with her mom's "mother's intuition"—for she'd witnessed the same sort of thing twice before with her brothers. With both Shane and Alec, Keeley's mom had told her dad—in secret, of course—on the very day she'd met each of the women they would eventually marry, that she'd known the minute she'd met Katelyn and Ariel that they'd be marrying Shane and Alec.

Hence, the more Keeley thought about her mother's past intuition, the more her heart swelled with hope—hope that maybe her mom had been right about Sutter the moment she'd seen him. Maybe Sutter really would be Keeley's husband someday.

"Was he a gentleman?" Joe asked Keeley, pulling her out of her spaced-out zoning mode and back to the conversation.

"Oh, of course, Dad," Keeley assured her father. She smiled, remembering how Sutter had suggested they tour his Lego room after they'd been kissing awhile on his sofa. "He's more...more—I don't know—more well-mannered, considerate...well, more everything good than any guy I've ever known."

"Are you already in love with him then?" Joe asked.

Keeley found she was holding her breath. He'd think she was nuts if she told him the truth—that, yes, she was in love with Sutter. Memories flashed through her mind—of her dad giving her the "you're just infatuated" talk when she was fifteen and thought she was in love with Travis Barry. Still, her parents had raised her with the "honesty is always the best policy" virtue.

And so she answered, "Yes. I know you think I'm crazy, Dad…but I'm not. It's so weird! I can't even explain it! It's like I've known him my whole life…or…or…"

"Or like you've been looking for him your whole life," Joe said, reaching to his left and taking Cynthia's hand in his. He winked at Cynthia, and Keeley noted the excess moisture that rose to her mother's eyes.

"Yeah," Keeley said, realizing that her father had put into words what she could not.

"Then be fearless, Keys," Joe counseled. "Don't doubt yourself or Sutter. Have confidence in your own feelings and intuitions…and in his, okay? People will scoff, tell you you're nuts, say you can't possibly be in love with him after such a short time. But ignore them, honey." Again he looked to Cynthia, leaned over, and kissed her on the mouth. "That's what we had to do, and we did it. And you know how happy your mom and I have always been. Through anything life throws at us, we've never doubted that we were meant for each other."

Keeley smiled, her heart swelling with confidence—assurance that all she felt for Sutter was genuine and true—that all he appeared to feel for her was just as sincere.

"Okay," she sighed. "Then that's what I'll do…be fearless." She paused a moment, looking from her father to her mother and back. "I know he's the one for me—that somehow I could never be as perfectly happy with anyone else as I will be with Sutter Price."

"I understand, baby," Cynthia said, brushing a tear from her cheek. "Believe me when I tell you that I truly do understand exactly what you're feeling."

Exhaling a sigh of relief and determination to soldier on no matter what the world might think, Keeley reached to the breadbasket in the center of the table and retrieved a slice of the delicious poppy seed bread. Taking a bite, she thought that, although it was delicious, she'd swap it in a heartbeat for one of Sutter's tasty kisses. She also thought that she was grateful she had wise and wonderful parents. How in all the world did she get so lucky in having them?

♥

"Well, I'm not surprised," Abby Price said as she chose another sugar cookie to begin decorating. "I mean, the way your eyes light up and you get that goofy grin every time you mention her...I figured she'd ruffled your bloomers."

"Men don't wear bloomers," Roy Price grumbled from his place in his recliner in the den.

Abby rolled her eyes, winking at her son.

"Mom," Sutter began, "I do not get a goofy grin every time I mention Keeley."

But Abby Price smiled—her smile that Sutter knew he'd inherited. Oh, he may have inherited his height and the color of his hair and eyes from his father, but everyone in the family said it was his mother's smile he smiled.

"Baby boy, I know you like the back of my hand," Abby stated. "Remember, you were in my womb for forty-one weeks and—"

"Nobody knows a boy better than his mother, yeah, yeah, yeah," Sutter chuckled. Smiling his mother's smile again, Sutter asked, "So you're telling me that you could tell this girl had me from the start?"

"She is," Roy said. "Anybody that knows you at all could tell it, son."

"Your dad's right, baby," his mother affirmed. "And there's nothing at all wrong with that." Setting down the cookie she'd just finished icing, Abby pushed the nearly empty bowl and beaters laced with green frosting toward Sutter where he sat on a stool at the island in the kitchen.

"Here, sweet pea…you wanna lick those beaters before I wash them?" she asked.

"Oh, for Pete's sake, Abby," Roy grumbled. "The boy's a grown man! He doesn't lick beaters anymore."

But Abby winked at Sutter and mouthed, *He's mad because he wanted to lick them.* Then picking up a bowl that still had a bit of blue frosting in it, she walked to her husband in his recliner. "I'm finished with the blue too, Roy…so stop sulking."

Sutter chuckled as his dad reached down, pulling on the recliner's lever and sitting up straight. Roy Price's eyes fairly sparkled as he accepted the frosting bowl from his wife.

"Thanks, Abbs," he said.

"You're such a goofball," Abby giggled, kissing her husband on the forehead before returning to the kitchen and her cookie decorating.

"Now, where were we?" she asked Sutter. "Oh yes…the De Carlo girl. So? What's your plan? Woo, win, and marry her?"

"Well, if you want the truth…yeah," Sutter admitted. There was no reason to keep them in the dark. They'd always trusted him—been supportive of everything he'd ever chosen to do or not to do—and he knew that would never change.

"Good," Roy interjected. " 'Cause I don't ever want that dipshidiot who broke through the ice on the lake coming here again. I'm still not convinced he's not going to try and sue us."

"Roy!" Abby scolded. "Your son is going to think that the only reason you're approving of his plans with this girl is because you don't want to get sued!"

"Oh, he knows I'm kidding, Abby," Roy mumbled. "Don't get your panties in a wad."

Sutter smiled—amused by his parents' playful banter. Although it might be misunderstood by outsiders, everyone in Sutter's family knew that Abby and Roy Price were like a comedy duo—playing off each other like professionals. It was a part of their relationship Sutter admired.

"The real question is," Roy began then, "does this girl know about your problem? Has she seen the Lego room?"

Nodding, Sutter answered, "Indeed she has, Dad. I showed it to her last night, after we went owling."

"Owling? Is that what they're calling it these days?" Roy teased, scraping one side of the frosting bowl with his index finger.

"In fact," Sutter continued, ignoring his dad's razzing, "we built a pretty impressive little tree house together. Keeley really knows her way around a bucket of random bricks."

"Well then, I guess that proves she's the one," Roy said, licking the blue frosting off his index finger.

"So even though I know you're being a smart ass, Dad...you guys are okay with me pursuing this girl all the way?" Sutter ventured.

Abby reached out and took Sutter's hands in her own. "Baby, you know we trust you and your decisions. You're a wise and wonderful man, sweet pea. If you love this girl, then of course...snatch her right up. The light in your eyes tells me that she will make you happy."

"Thanks, Mom," Sutter said. He loved his mom. She got him; she'd always gotten him.

"Dad?" he asked, turning to look at his father.

Roy Price licked some blue frosting off his index finger again. "Well, if it'll keep us from getting sued by that idiot that went into the lake..."

"Roy! Be serious," Abby scolded.

Getting up from his recliner, Roy swaggered over to the kitchen sink, depositing his frosting bowl into it and rinsing his hands. Drying them with the dishtowel he'd pulled off of the refrigerator door handle, he said, "You're a good man, son. You know I'm proud of you and who you are. If you like this girl, then you go get her. And don't let some dipshidiot who doesn't know his butt from his elbow get in your way…family reunion or not."

"Okay," Sutter agreed.

He watched as his dad spun the dishtowel into a towel whip. He knew he probably should've warned his mom, but the truth was, Sutter liked watching his parents flirt. And when Abby Price turned around to begin icing another sugar cookie, Roy Price winked at his son and snapped the dishtowel whip, hitting his wife smartly on the right bum cheek.

"Ow!" Abby yelped. "Roy! I'll have a welt for a week!" she scolded, rubbing her right bum cheek.

"Aw, don't be mad, baby," Roy said. "Come here…I'll kiss it and make it better."

"Roy Price! Don't you dare!" Abby squealed, quickly wiping her hands on her apron before sprinting off toward the den.

"Come here, sugar!" Roy teased, running after her. "Let me take that sting off it a bit."

As Sutter watched his parents tumble into his dad's recliner and begin kissing, he smiled—for it was exactly something he could imagine Keeley and him doing someday. Only he would never dishtowel-whip Keeley as sharply as his dad always did his mom. Sutter vowed in that moment that he would never do anything to hurt Keeley, the woman he loved—never.

♥

Keeley startled just a little when she heard the knock on the door. Still, Sutter had texted her, asking if he could drop by for a minute before she left for the Christmas Eve dinner with her family. Of course, she suggested they meet at the secret little cabin behind the lodge. Not only would it ensure their privacy, but also it was so close to the lodge that she could leave at the very last minute to arrive promptly—ensuring she could spend more time with Sutter.

"Hi," she greeted when she opened the door to see boom-boom-foxy Sutter Price standing there.

"Hi," he said, smiling at her. "Do you have time for me to come in for a minute?"

Keeley arched one eyebrow alluringly. Or at least she hoped it was alluringly—that it didn't just make her look stupid.

"Do I have time for you to come in for a minute?" she asked. Then brazenly reaching out and taking hold of the front of his barn coat, she pulled him over the threshold and into the house.

Chuckling, Sutter slammed the door closed behind him and then stripped off his beanie and gloves before gathering Keeley into his arms and claiming her mouth with his own. Oh, how Keeley loved the scent of him—the feel of being in his arms! As her heart beat madly with love, desire, and happiness in knowing she'd found the one man who could make her happy, she wondered how she'd ever leave him when the family reunion was over. But the moment was too wonderful, and she wouldn't let worry and anxiety taint it.

Blissful in his arms, enraptured by his kiss, the thought flittered through Keeley's mind, *He really does taste better than poppy seed bread!*

CHAPTER NINE

Although Keeley tried to be mentally present at the Christmas Eve dinner, it proved very difficult. All she could think about was Sutter—finishing dinner so she could be with Sutter, finishing the family games so she could be with Sutter. Oh, not that she didn't enjoy all the fun and games—especially the Ring on a String game, when Paisley had beat the pants off Judd three times in a row. Of course, she almost immediately felt guilty for delighting in Judd's losses. After all, most of the members of the De Carlo family had been playing Ring on a String since childhood. It was a game that spanned generations, a game with a simple pretext: a string anchored to a ceiling on one end, with a round metal ring on the other, was held by the player who let it go or pushed it at a hook anchored on a wall. Successfully hitting the hook with the ring and hearing the "clank" awarded the player certain points. But the grand accomplishment each player hoped for was to actually ring the hook. And it was the last game scheduled for the Christmas Eve festivities. Therefore, not only did Keeley find some guilty pleasure in Paisley's skill dominating Judd's where the game was concerned, but also it signaled the official end of the De Carlo family reunion Christmas Eve. Soon everyone else would head back to their individual family cabins. Soon Keeley could be with Sutter again.

And almost as if her thoughts had summoned him, Sutter entered the game room of the lodge, just as everyone was saying good night.

"Did you all have fun?" he asked, going to the fireplace and stirring the embers. "Were you warm enough?"

"Oh yes!" Cynthia assured him. "This is a wonderful place, Sutter. Just wonderful!"

"And Mom says that Santa will come…even way out here!" Paisley exclaimed.

"Oh, definitely!" Sutter assured her. "In fact, we were just watching the news in the office, and NORAD has been tracking Santa for over ten hours already! He's set to hit Idaho about three a.m., they say."

"Yay!" Paisley squealed with delight. "I hope I can get to sleep before he comes!"

"Oh, you've got five whole hours to get to sleep," Sutter offered. "I'm sure you'll make it."

"Don't be so certain," Joe sighed as Paisley began dancing in circles around him.

"I guess we all better get to bed, if we want to be asleep before Santa comes," Keeley's aunt Krystal suggested.

Everyone began hugging and saying their good nights in agreement. In fact, Keeley was feeling so elated at the prospect of the family finally scattering so she could spend some more time in Sutter's company that her happy heart even found renewed patience with Judd. And as he approached her, arms spread in indicating he was going to hug her, she softened toward him, smiling in welcoming not Judd necessarily but the end of ever having to worry about his awkward pushiness toward her again.

"Merry Christmas, Keeley," he said, embracing her.

"Merry Christmas, Judd," she returned, noting how scrawny his body and arms felt in comparison to those she'd been held in and against just hours before—Sutter's.

Nevertheless, Keeley had let down her guard. Bathed in the felicity of knowing hours spent in Sutter's company were now just minutes away, Keeley was not prepared to defend herself from anything unexpected—especially Judd forcing a kiss to her mouth.

Holding her breath and struggling to push herself from his arms, Keeley found that Judd was unexpectedly much stronger than he looked. His arms banded around her like a vise grip as his mouth mushed to hers in a wet, slimy sort of kiss that turned her stomach— stimulated her gag reflex.

"What the hell, man?" she heard Sutter shout.

"Judd, man! What are you doing?" Ethan hollered.

"Let her go!" It was Sutter's voice again. And as Keeley struggled, trying to escape—as she thought she might throw up from the feel of and knowledge that Judd Sutherland was kissing her—she found she was suddenly liberated, as she felt her father rip her from Judd's clutches as Sutter threw her assailant to the floor.

"What the hell is wrong with you?" Sutter shouted. "You don't put your hands on her!"

Surprisingly, Judd sprang to his feet, shouting, "You don't tell me what to do, farm boy! You shouldn't even be here! You're not family!"

"Neither are you, jackass!" Sutter growled. He ducked, avoiding the fist Judd threw at him. "Believe me, man…you do not want to go there with me."

But Judd swung again. Sutter ducked, throwing a lethal punch to Judd's midsection, and when Judd doubled over in pain, Sutter put a foot in his chest, shoving him backward and causing him to land on his butt on the floor.

"Take it easy, boys," Joe said.

Keeley watched as her father put a hand on Sutter's shoulder—as Ethan and his brother, Ricky, helped Judd to stand.

"Not cool, man," Ethan grumbled.

"You shouldn't have allowed him to come, Krystal," Uncle Tony said to his wife.

"No kidding," Krystal mumbled.

"This is your fault, Ethan," Ricky began to accuse. "You know Judd's been hot for Keeley for years! What? You think he wanted to come just to hang out with our family?"

"Wait…please," Keeley said, however. Looking to Sutter—remembering what he'd so wisely told her about being straightforward with people—she looked at each of the De Carlo family members. "This is my fault," she began. And although everyone began to protest—including and especially Sutter—she held up one hand to beg them to listen to her. Then looking to Judd, facing him squarely, she began, "I don't know what else I could've done, Judd. I never have said yes when you've asked me out. I've tried in every way, except for just telling you straight out that…that…I just am not interested in you, Judd. I never have been, and I never will be, and I'm sorry if I ever gave you any indication at all that I would be. I…I should've told you a long time ago—years ago—but I didn't want to hurt your feelings. But now I realize how stupid I was, because in the end…" She glanced to Sutter, and he winked at her with reassurance. "In the end, somehow you thought I would come around or something. And here you are, at our family reunion, when you shouldn't be…and thinking that because I've been so nice, there must be some possibility that I'll—I don't know—change my feelings about you. But I won't, Judd. You're a really nice guy, most of the time. But I don't like you that way. I never will. Not ever. So please stop trying. And don't ever touch me again."

Judd glared at Keeley, growling, "You're just a tease, that's all. You led me on!"

Sutter lurched forward, but Joe caught hold of his arm. "She's fighting her own battle, son. Let her do it…at least this time, okay?"

Keeley could see the firm set of Sutter's jaw—that he wanted to beat the tar out of Judd. But instead, he gritted his teeth and nodded at her with encouragement.

"I did not, and you know it," Keeley defended herself. "I admit that I was too nice to you, that I should've told you flat out that I would never date you, ever…but that's all. I never led you on, and you know it."

Judd, humiliated and furious, glanced around the room to the members of the De Carlo family. "You're all a bunch of psychos. I'm outta here!" he bellowed. Then Judd Sutherland turned and stormed out of the lodge.

As Krystal started to go after him, Tony stalled her. "He brought his own car. Let him get his stuff and leave," he said.

"I'm sorry, Keeley," Krystal said, brushing tears from her eyes. "I'm sorry, everyone! I'm so sorry."

"It's not your fault, Mom," Ethan said. "I shouldn't have bought Judd's pitiful story." Going to Keeley, Ethan hugged her. "I'm so sorry, Keys. Honestly."

"It's not your fault, Ethan," Keeley assured him, returning her cousin's hug. "I should've been honest a long time ago. It's really not your fault."

"I'm so sorry, Paisley," she heard Sutter say.

Turning around, she saw Paisley sniffling, Sutter hunkered down in front of her.

"I shouldn't have been so mean to Judd," Sutter said. Taking Paisley's little hands in his own, he continued, "I...I should've talked to him calmly and—"

"No! No, Sutter!" Paisley wept, however. "You saved Keeley! You saved her! She did *not* want to kiss Judd. I'm just very, very mad that he kissed Keeley! I'm so glad you saved her!"

Throwing her arms around Sutter's neck, Paisley sobbed into his shoulder. As Keeley watched Sutter comforting her little sister, her heart powerfully reaffirmed that she already loved Sutter and knew that her love for him would grow with every passing moment.

"Keys? Are you okay?" Paisley asked, releasing Sutter and turning to look up at her big sister.

"Of course, Paiz," Keeley assured her sister. "No worries, okay?"

Sniffling, Paisley offered, "Mom brought the peroxide if you need to get the facteeria from Judd off your face."

Everyone chuckled, tenderly amused by Paisley's caring suggestion.

"Okay," Keeley said. "I'll keep that in mind."

Nodding, Paisley then turned to Sutter, cupped her hand around his ear, and whispered something to him.

Smiling, Sutter said, "I think that's a great idea, Paisley. I'll hitch up Stackhouse right now. And then tomorrow morning, after Santa has come and you've opened all your presents, I'll take you on another sleigh ride, okay? Christmas morning sleigh rides are the best sleigh rides ever. We can even sing Good King Wince's Snot too, if you like, okay?"

Paisley nodded and then looked to Keeley. "Sutter said he will take you on a sleigh ride to help you feel better, okay, Keys?"

Keeley smiled at her little kindhearted sister and then at the man she was hopelessly and blissfully in love with. "Okay," she said.

"Well, this is a Christmas Eve we won't soon forget," Joe sighed. "How about we all hit the hay, remember only the good stuff about tonight, and start fresh tomorrow, huh?"

"Sounds like a good idea," Krystal agreed.

Rising to his feet, Sutter walked to Keeley. Reaching out and taking her face between his hands, he said, "I'll text you when I've got Stackhouse hitched up to the sleigh, okay?"

"Okay," Keeley said.

And then—to her delighted astonishment—Sutter kissed her—leaned forward, placing a long, loving kiss to her lips before releasing her, saying, "You all have a good night. Merry Christmas!" and heading out of the lodge's game room.

Turning, Keeley saw twenty-something sets of widened eyes staring at her and twenty-something mouths gaping open in astonishment. Of course, her own mom and dad weren't surprised. Rather they stood looking at her with nothing but love and approval in their expressions.

Keeley shrugged, offering, "This turned out to be my favorite family reunion yet."

"And I bet boom-boom-foxy's kiss was way better tasting than mean old Judd's kiss, huh, Keys?" Paisley offered.

As everyone began shooting questions at her parents concerning how on earth their oldest daughter had managed to get to know Sutter well enough to be kissing him already, Keeley knelt down, gathering Paisley into her arms and hugging her tightly.

"Oh, definitely, Paiz," Keeley answered. "Definitely!"

♥

Joe and Cynthia De Carlo sat on the back porch of Snow Creek's Cozy Cabin. The sound of sleigh bells was faint but still audible somewhere in the distance.

As Cynthia sipped her mug of hot chocolate, Joe stared into the fire burning in the small fireplace at the far end of the porch.

"She won't be coming home with us, will she, babe?" he asked his wife.

"No, I don't think she will," Cynthia confirmed, exhaling a melancholy sigh. "Of course, she'll come home at some point to pack up and move out of her apartment, I'm sure—you know, to plan the wedding and things."

"I know," Joe mumbled. "But I mean…this is it, isn't it? This is the guy I've been praying would find her all her life…and yet dreading the day that he would."

"Yes, honey, it's him," Cynthia whispered, dabbing at a tear that trickled over her cheek.

"The kid's a good man," Joe said, his eyes moist with emotion.

"An exceptional man, Joe," Cynthia concurred. Then, gazing at him, she added, "Just like you. He'll make her happy…the way I've been since the day we met."

"I hope so," Joe said, exhaling another heavy sigh.

He was surprised when Cynthia unexpectedly began to giggle in spite of her tears.

"What's so funny?" he asked.

Cynthia shook her head and then answered, "Paisley…asking Keeley if she wanted the peroxide so she could get Judd's 'facteeria' off her face."

The heaviness in Joe's heart lessened a little, and he smiled. "One thing about Paisley…she'll keep us young."

"If we're lucky," Cynthia added.

Looking to Cynthia, Joe winked at her, saying, "We are lucky, sugar. For some reason, we always have been."

"Luck. Or blessed. Either way, life has been wonderful…because I have you," Cynthia softly said.

"Hey," Joe began, attempting to lighten their mood a bit more, "what's say we do a bit of owling, hmm?"

"Is that what they're calling it now days?" Cynthia giggled.

Setting her mug down on the porch floor, she stood up, walked to her husband, and kissed him passionately.

"I love you, Cynthia," Joe mumbled, pulling her onto his lap.

"I love you too, Joe," she said.

"Now what do you say we get back to some owling, hmm?" Joe De Carlo mumbled against his wife's soft lips.

Oh, it was a beautiful Christmas Eve! Keeley closed her eyes a moment, thinking back on the way the frost fell through the clear, cold, midnight sky to land on her eyelashes and cheeks as Stackhouse had pulled the sleigh along. She'd never known a more enchanted, dreamlike night. The moon was full and bright and sat high in the sky like a crystal-lit, incandescent ornament meant to light their way. The snow and frost on the ground were smooth and unmarred, holding captive the silvery moonlight, further illuminating their way. And as Stackhouse's bells jingled in rhythm to his trot, Keeley had snuggled up against Sutter's warm body.

"I'm just glad you weren't angry with me," Sutter said as he returned from the kitchen carrying a large bowl of freshly popped popcorn.

"For what?" Keeley asked as he sat down next to her on the sofa, placing the popcorn bowl on the steamer trunk in front of them.

"For losing my cool again with that dipshidiot of yours," he explained.

Keeley giggled. "He's not my dipshidiot, remember? And anyway, why would I be angry with you for defending my honor?"

Sutter smiled, shrugging broad shoulders. "I don't know. I guess I'm just worried something will make you change your mind about me."

"Believe me," Keeley said, leaning forward and gathering a handful of popcorn out of the bowl, "nothing could ever make me change my mind about you."

"Is that so?" Sutter inquired, putting an arm around her shoulders as she leaned back against the sofa.

"I promise," Keeley assured him as she snuggled up against him. "And are you proud of me for taking your advice...even if it was belatedly?"

"My advice?" Sutter asked.

"Yes! Remember when you told me that sometimes trying not to hurt someone's feelings is worse than just telling them straight out? Well, it took Judd being a total...a total..."

"Dipshidiot? Jackass?" Sutter suggested.

"Both," Keeley laughed. "It took him assaulting me to make me realize you were right. I should've told him long ago that...that..."

"To sled down into a lake?" Sutter chuckled.

Keeley giggled. "Exactly!"

"Well, I am proud of you," Sutter admitted. "I know how hard it was for you to do that...being that you are a *foxy* INFP and all."

Keeley exhaled a relieved and contented sigh. "But it's over now, and I'm here with you...and that's all that matters to me."

"It's all that matters to me too," he said, kissing the top of her head.

She loved the feel of being with Sutter—of being next to him—touching him. He looked so handsome sitting there on the sofa in his jeans, red socks, and ecru long underwear shirt.

The sleigh ride they'd enjoyed together earlier had certainly been magical, but in those late, quiet, Christmas Eve moments, Keeley much preferred to be snuggling warm and cozy on Sutter's sofa, a fire blazing in the hearth. It had begun snowing almost the moment they'd returned from the sleigh ride, and now, as Keeley glanced out through the large picture window on the far side of the room, she sighed with further contentment. The snow was still falling—not blowing but falling, drifting down in large, fluffy tufts of snowflakes that clung together like frosted fairies holding hands. Keeley thought to herself that she wished she and Sutter could linger in that moment forever—in the soft calm of the cabin, the fire crackling in the hearth, and their arms around one another. She knew she was lingering in a truly perfect space in time, and she savored it.

Sutter knew he was crazy. Every ounce of common sense in him—and his parents had always maintained Sutter had more common sense than anyone on earth—murmured in his head, telling him he was nuts. He'd known the girl, what—seventy-two hours? And yet his heart was beating so hard inside his chest that he was more certain with each passing second that he should do it—not to wait—just take the plunge before his common sense convinced him otherwise.

Of course, another part of him didn't want to move at all! Lounging there on the sofa in front of the fire with Keeley snuggled up against him—it was like walking through heaven and never wanting to leave. But as his heart began to race, urging him to do what he wanted to do more than anything he'd ever wanted to do in all his life, Sutter reached forward with his free hand, fisting some popcorn in it.

"Oops," he mumbled as he intentionally dropped several kernels of the popcorn onto the sofa and Keeley's lap. "Will the butter leave a stain, do you think?" he asked, feigning innocence.

"Maybe we better be safe," Keeley said as she began picking up the scattered kernels of popcorn.

Making certain that when Keeley shifted her position, several more kernels fell between two of the sofa's cushions, Sutter said, "Oh, great...now I've made it worse, and they're really down in there."

"We'll get them," Keeley brightly assured him.

"Your hands are smaller," Sutter offered. "Can you reach down there between these two cushions and make sure we got it all?"

"Of course," Keeley said. He watched as she dug between the cushions. "Here's one," she said, pulling out an unpopped kernel and handing it to him. "Uh oh...and another," she said as she found another one of the unpopped kernels Sutter had previously planted between the two cushions while Keeley was in the bathroom following their sleigh ride.

"Oh, wait. Wait...there's something else down here," Keeley said.

Sutter held his breath—watched as an expression of being perplexed crossed her pretty face.

"I don't think it's popcorn though," she informed him. "It actually feels like something else...like maybe a...a...a ring."

Sutter continued to hold his breath as he watched Keeley pull the engagement ring from between the couch cushions.

Keeley's heart leapt for a moment as she studied the beautiful, vintage-looking engagement ring she'd dug out of Sutter's couch. Her first emotion was elation, thinking that the gorgeous boom-boom-foxy man she'd been sharing popcorn with had actually hidden the ring in the sofa as an unfathomably romantic way in which to begin a proposal. Almost instantly, however, reality struck, and she wondered if perhaps the ring had belonged to some other girl—a girl who had won Sutter's heart sometime in the past—and that she had lost the ring between the cushions of the couch.

"Is…is this yours?" she asked, holding the ring out toward Sutter—uncertain as to whether her heart was breaking or beginning its ascent to cloud nine.

But then Sutter Price—who had only a moment before been standing in front of her between the couch and steamer trunk coffee table—dropped to one knee, saying, "No, it's yours…if…if you want it…if you want to marry me, Keeley De Carlo. Will you marry me, Keeley? I know you must think I've lost my mind. You've only known me a matter of days, but I—"

"Yes!" Keeley squealed, bursting into tears of joy as her heart soared to cloud nine on the rocket fuel that was her thoroughgoing, all-consuming, and infinite love for Sutter!

"You will?" Sutter breathed, smiling.

Keeley giggled, for he looked as if he weren't certain she would say yes.

"Yes!" she cried as more tears sprang from her eyes to moisten her cheeks. "Yes, Sutter! Yes!"

Almost leaping to his feet and pulling her off the couch and into his arms, Sutter kissed her mouth first and then her neck, whispering, "I love you, Keeley. I knew it was you…from the moment I first saw you."

"And I knew it was you too," Keeley wept against his shoulder. "I love you, Sutter! I think I always have...even before we met."

Kissing her again, Sutter sighed, and Keeley again thought it strange that he would even consider she would refuse him.

"Now, we can get you another ring next week if you like," he said, releasing her, taking the ring from her, and slipping it easily onto her left ring finger. "This was my great-grandmother's ring. She gave it to me before she passed away because I was always so mesmerized by it when I was a kid. So if you don't want this one, we can—"

"I love it, Sutter!" Keeley interrupted, brushing tears from her eyes as she studied the beautiful art deco white gold engagement ring. It was a beautiful piece with a European-cut diamond as the center stone and a spray of five tiny diamonds fanning out over the top of it.

"It has a companion wedding band with five more little ones that nestle up against the bottom of the middle stone," Sutter explained. "But I really want you to have what you want, Keeley. So I'm not going to be offended if you don't want my—"

Sutter smiled as Keeley threw her arms around his neck, kissing his cheek and weeping with joy as she whispered into his ear, "It means so much more to me that it was your great-grandmother's, Sutter. I think you know that, don't you?"

"I admit that I thought it would," he confessed. Placing a lingering kiss to her neck first, Sutter then asked, "You're not going to leave day after tomorrow, are you? I mean, I know you have a job, probably a place of your own. But I'm hoping you can work from here a bit and will stay for a while. You won't leave me quite yet, will you?"

Pulling back to gaze into his gorgeous green-blue eyes—still stunned to dizziness by what was happening—Keeley answered, "I never want to leave you ever again, Sutter. And I can't think of anything I'm even willing to go home and pack up if it means being separated from you. And you're right. I can work from anywhere! It's the biggest perk of my job, actually. So, no, if you want me here, I'll stay with you…and never leave again."

Sutter smiled at her, gathered her against the warm strength of his body, and administered such an impassioned, heated kiss to her that dizziness did overpower her for several seconds—but only several. And then, wrapping her arms around his neck, she returned his kiss with as much yearning and desire as he offered to her.

When Sutter broke the seal of their lips a moment, Keeley looked up to him, smiling.

"What's so funny?" Sutter asked, gazing down at her with love smoldering in his gorgeous eyes.

"Just thinking of what Paisley said when you came walking out of the office to greet us when we arrived," she admitted.

"And what did she say?" Sutter asked, taking her face in his hands and tracing her lower lip with one thumb.

"Boom-boom-foxy," she answered.

"What?" he chuckled.

"I'll explain later," Keeley promised. "But for now, tell me again that you love me so I'll know I'm not dreaming all this."

Sutter grinned an entirely seductive grin, the intonation of his voice as provocative as his smile, when he said, "I love you, Keeley. And you're not dreaming."

And as the tufts of frosted fairies continued to tumble from the sky—as the fire popped and crackled in the hearth—Sutter persisted in telling Keeley he loved her—with words and with such sublime kisses that Christmas Eve began to slumber—and Christmas Day awoke.

EPILOGUE

"You're sure you're not too cold, baby?" Sutter asked Keeley.

"I'm sure," Keeley assured him. "The fire is keeping me nice and toasty warm."

Inhaling deeply of the cold night air, Keeley savored the rustic comfort of the wood smoke and the feel of frost in the air. Taking a sip of hot chocolate from her mug, she sighed with contentment. She could hardly believe it had been an entire year since she first set eyes on Sutter—could hardly believe they'd been married for eight months already. And as she sat next to Sutter on the back porch of their cabin, listening to the fire crackle and the sound of Stackhouse's bells somewhere off in the distance, she hoped time wouldn't always slip by so quickly. Yet she knew that moments like the one she was lingering in then—those private moments of solitude she and Sutter enjoyed together—were what she needed to focus on, not the others that sped by at the speed of light.

"I guess Dad really is taking Mom 'owling' tonight," Sutter said, making quotation marks with his fingers.

"Good thing Stackhouse's bells don't scare away the owls on the kind of 'owling' your dad likes to do," Keeley giggled.

Sutter smiled. "I'm glad they took the sleigh out. They rarely get to use it on Christmas Eve anymore—at least for just the two of them. The guests just like the sleigh rides too much."

"Well, speaking as one who has been a guest at Snow Creek, a Christmas Eve sleigh ride *is* a truly magical experience," Keeley offered.

"Oh, is it now?" Sutter asked.

"It surely is," Keeley assured him, kissing him softly on the mouth. "And I'm so glad we visited with my family last week so that we could be home, just us, tonight…and tomorrow."

"Me too," Sutter agreed.

"You make all of my happiness, you know, Sutter Price," Keeley whispered, snuggling up against him on the wooden swing they shared.

"Well, *you* are my happiness too, you know. You're my everything, Keeley Price," Sutter countered. "You're my lover, my wife, my friend. I guess you could say you're the ultimate Lego to me."

Keeley laughed. "Wow! The ultimate Lego, huh? You really do love me!"

"You know it," he teased. "We fit together perfectly, just like two Legos. You build them with me too, and you know what they say…"

"No. What do they say?" Keeley asked, delighted by Sutter's analogy.

"They say the couple that builds Legos together stays together— which I think is very appropriate since in truth it can be almost impossible to separate two Lego bricks sometimes, you know."

"Oh, I do know," Keeley said. Reaching up, she slipped her finger under Sutter's top lip, gently rubbing his top left incisor. "And you've got a veneer over a chipped tooth to prove it."

"Yes, I do," Sutter chuckled. "But better me than you. And that was a freaking awesome medieval castle we built this summer. Well worth a trip to the dentist."

"If you say so, Boom-Boom," Keeley giggled. She sipped her hot chocolate and then set the mug down on the floor of the porch next to the swing.

"Where do you think Santa is about now?" she asked Sutter.

"Oh, probably scrambling to find that Jack Sparrow Funko Pop Paisley asked for," he answered, smiling.

"I have it on good authority that he's already taken care of that," Keeley assured him.

"Well, in that case, he's probably breathing a sigh of relief and chowing down some fortune cookies in China or something." Sutter paused and then asked, "And what do you want for Christmas, little girl?"

"You," Keeley said, raising her head from Sutter's shoulder and kissing him on the neck. "You…just to be alone with you."

"You've got it," Sutter said, kissing her tenderly on the mouth. "And maybe we can work in a little owling tomorrow night, if you like." He kissed her again.

"Is that what they're calling it these days?" Keeley breathed against Sutter's lips.

"From what I hear, yeah," Sutter mumbled, gathering his wife into his arms.

"Then owling it is," Keeley whispered as her husband's mouth descended over hers—claimed hers—ravaged hers with such a loving hunger she could hardly breathe.

"Merry Christmas, Keys," Sutter said.

"Merry Christmas, Boom-Boom," Keeley giggled as Sutter stood up, whisking her into the cradle of his arms.

"Let the owling commence," he chuckled as he carried her into their warm and cozy cabin—into their haven from winter—into their private, loving wonderland.

AUTHOR'S NOTE

Each year during autumn, I find myself wanting to write Christmassy things. It's one reason I've usually got a wintery or Christmassy book being released just before Thanksgiving or Christmas. And this year wasn't much different, other than the fact that the unhappiness and anger and inability to truly enjoy autumn and Christmastime I've been battling for so many years has lifted. It took me up until the very end of this book, writing the last three chapters, to realize why.

Even as a tiny little kid, I loved Christmas! My dad always tells a story about how I would start gift-wrapping rocks in July in preparation for Christmas gift giving. Christmas has lived in my heart year-round for as long as I can remember. And yet, thinking back, beginning in 2005, Christmas had ceased to be enjoyable for me. It took everything I could muster to put on the happy Mrs. Santa Claus face and fake the joy that had once been so deep and sincere in my heart and spirit. Oh, I never really told anybody—not for years and years anyway. And lots of times circumstances or events surrounding Christmastime (i.e., obligations that were demanded of me and my family, bad weather, running our own business and all the stress that goes with it, and having my kids leave home one by one as they grew up) were the reasons I thought my joy was gone.

But when, during the writing and publication process of *Romance in a Winter Wonderland*, I began to notice that my heart wasn't so angry all the time and that I was even experiencing moments of joy and excitement about the season, I began to slowly realize what had changed: my mom had moved from this life to the next and was no longer in pain, confusion, despair, and agony.

My mom *loved* Christmas! She loved that the world celebrated and acknowledged the birth of the Savior, and she truly carried Christ in her heart every minute of every day. Mom always made Christmas so special—baking things she didn't bake at any other time of the year and making sure there were heartfelt gifts waiting under our tree and the trees of her folks, sister, and brothers. Every year my sister and I would make a pretty paper chain out of red and green ribbon, and Mom would proudly display it on our mantel and around our fireplace. Decorating the tree was a wonderful time together for our family, filled with lots of laughter and reminiscing over the history of certain ornaments. Dad would get up at three a.m. Christmas morning and build a fire in the fireplace to begin warming up our cozy little house, and no matter how tired Mom was from being up so late helping Santa, she was always quick to rise from her bed, her eyes twinkling as she watched my sister and I delight in Christmas morning.

But for so many years now (fourteen, if I count from when I personally began noticing something was wrong with Mom's memory and things), Christmas has been an unhappy time for me because it was unhappy for my mom. Her heart began to break and wither as her illnesses progressed, and during the last couple of years of her life, she wasn't even comprehending that there was a Christmas, let alone what it was. And as I was writing this book—as my heart was a whole lot happier in thinking of Christmas and the birth of our Savior—I slowly began to realize that it is because my mother's understanding of, love for, and joy in Christmas and all it represents is restored to her—that now she's like Clarence in *It's a Wonderful Life*, having a knowledge beyond ours here. I know Mom is now lingering with such a joy in having her mind restored and being with loved ones she has missed for so long, that Christmas this year has at last begun to feel like Christmases felt before 2005—and I'm able to focus on enjoying time with my husband, children, grandchildren, and intimate friends in a way I haven't been able to in so long. I even realized that this is the first year since 2006 that I've been able to truly "see" my Christmas tree! Now the pretty colored lights and glass balls look beautiful beyond explanation to me and serve to soothe my tired mind and soul the way Christmas trees did before my mom began drowning in the terrifying confusion and fear of dementia and Alzheimer's disease. Furthermore, an experience and gift of the very tender mercy kind touched my heart during the course of writing this book. I pause to share it, because it's personal to me, but 'tis the season of the celebration of the Savior's birth, and what are we without the Savior and his great sacrifice? So I will share the quick version of the experience with you, in hopes that it will buoy you up in some small way, as it buoyed me up tremendously.

It has been a rough year, fraught with great loss, accompanied by great emotional, physical, and other sorts of pain. But a few weeks ago, as Kevin and I sat in the den one night discussing how on earth we were going to keep the business afloat, keep our spirits up, and find the strength to persevere, we agreed to pull ourselves up by the bootstraps, get up the next morning, and hit the ground running again. We determined we were going to enjoy the holidays, spend more time with our family members, and get back to finding joy in life each and every day, instead of letting the weight of everything we were yoked with pull us down.

Well, the next morning, I woke up and looked at the clock to see that it was about seven a.m. This is a very late hour for the old me to be waking up—but about average for new me who has been so stressed and heartbroken these past few years. I looked at the clock again and remembered the conversation Kevin and I had had the night before.

I closed my eyes and thought to myself, Can I do it? I'm not sure I can do it. Maybe I'll just lie here for a while and get up later. Maybe I'll feel better if I lie here a while longer.

Now we all know that there is nothing that drags you down and starts your day off on the wrong foot like lingering in bed too long in the morning, right? But it was a habit I was beginning to develop—and, worse, give in to.

So there I was with my eyes closed, planning on trying to snooze a bit longer—"Get up! And be happy!"

My eyes popped open, and I half expected to see my mom standing there right next to my bed, smiling down at me with her bright and happy morning smile the way she'd always done when I was little. Mom had just told me to get up and be happy! And I know some will say it was my imagination. Some will say it was the Spirit speaking to me—and it may have been the Spirit, and it if was, I know my mother was standing there telling the Spirit what to tell me to get me to listen. But this I do know: I was wide awake, and I heard my mother say, "Get up! And be happy!" and I knew exactly what she meant.

Hopping out of bed, I knew I would have to work at being happy that day. But that's a fact we all face most of the time, isn't it? I quickly got ready for the day and went about trying to finish all the things that needed to be finished. And even though I knew I'd never get everything done that needed getting done that day, I had my mother's strength with me again—the strength to push forward, get busy, accomplish what I could accomplish, and live and be happy.

You may be thinking this is a little heavy for an Author's Note at the end of a fluffy, feel-good romance novella, but it's part of this book—written in every line, emotion, and descriptive sentence—and I thought you should know, so that you will know me even better than you did before.

Now, after all that seriousness, of course I have some fun trivia snippets for you. But before those, I'm also going to share something else very personal with you. Below are seven little Christmas-themed excerpts taken from things my mom wrote. I cherish them so much, and they take me back to a simpler time when "things" weren't so important and every gift was a treasure to be remembered for a lifetime. I cherish these little insights into my mom's childhood rural Christmases, her young mother Christmases, and even my own (I'm the Skeeter/Marcia she mentions)—and I hope you will enjoy them, as well.

Merry Christmas, My Darling!
Marcia Lynn McClure

1. Darkness would have set in before I got off the bus at night. I sometimes would walk from the bus stop to home on the snowplowed road with the moonlight glistening on the snow on both sides. Before I reached the driveway, I would smell fresh-baked bread, the cinnamon of fresh-baked sweet rolls, and pinto beans cooking. Ahh! There's not a person on earth who ever ate so well on a cold wintry night. For my after-school snack, Mom

would let me have a small bowl of beans with lots of black pepper and a glass of good, cold, uncooked (unpasteurized) whole milk. Christmas is in the air.

2. The attic was a neat place to sneak away to for a little privacy (especially since I didn't have a window seat). One Christmas season when I was still very young, I came home from school, slipped up to the attic, and made red and green construction paper chains. (Yes, Skeeter, we had construction paper when I was young.) I was having so much fun I hardly noticed I had turned into a block of ice until Mom found me.

3. Christmases were great fun at our house. Santa Claus bought us each a nice gift and filled our stockings with oranges, candy, and nuts. Mom and Dad always gave us each a couple of small gifts, usually clothes and some little trinket.

4. The Christmas of 1954, my senior year, I got a Lane cedar chest, which I still have. Sharon got a piano, which she still has, Wayne got a .22 rifle, and Russell got a pair of boots, a black cowboy outfit, and a toy gun belt with two holsters and toy guns. After Dad started managing the Lemon's Feed Score, he got a bonus twice a year, one of which was around Christmas. This year I'm sure most if not all of his bonus went for Christmas. I don't know how much they paid for my cedar chest, but I do know Sharon's piano was ninety dollars.

5. Other gifts I remember receiving from my parents are two Shirley Temple books and *Patty O'Neal on the Airways*, which I still have. Another book they gave me at some time was *The Swiss Family Robinson*. These may have been birthday gifts. These are the only books I ever remember owning until recent years except for my scriptures and some church books and *The Little Red Hen*, which Aunt Opal gave me while we were still at Westcliffe.

6. Other Christmas gifts I remember receiving are a Bible, which I requested, a jewelry box, a string of "pearls," and a pink sweater set. The last three were all received at one Christmas, I think in 1953. Normally, we never received a lot of gifts like so many do today, but it was a lot to us. I also have the remains of a big baby doll that still cries but whose two front teeth have fallen inside. She also has a broken leg. My sister stepped on it. Guess I should have kept her off the attic floor. (This is me, Marcia…and I have to tell you how much I giggle whenever I read the sentence "I have the remains of a big baby doll" written here by Mom! It's so her! And so me! "The remains"—sounds like she read one too many police novels, hmm? And just so you know, I now possess the remains of my mom's baby doll—and other than her leg that slips off, she is quite intact, especially for a composition doll from that era.)

7. Christmastime came. Oris, Marcia, Luanna, and I, all in the front seat of the pickup, made a trip to Pocatello to get the J.C. Penney order. Marcia received a vanity set with the stool filled with all kinds of candy from Santa. She wanted a pair of purple velvet pants and a body suit. The closest I could come was a white body suit, a pair of purple uncut corduroy pants, and a turquoise suede belt with a wide brass buckle. She was happy. She recently told me it was her favorite outfit ever. (Marcia again—and it was my favorite outfit ever! I still have the pants and belt!)

Snippet #1—Keeley's last name was inspired by one of my favorite silver-screen actresses, Yvonne De Carlo. If you're familiar with her at all, it's probably from the old TV show *The Munsters*. She was Lily Munster, Herman Munster's rather vampire-ish-looking wife and the mother of their son, Eddie. But I always think of her first as Moses's

(Charlton Heston's) wife, Sephora, in MGM's incredible 1954 production of *The Ten Commandments*! Oh, she was a classic beauty, wasn't she?

Snippet #2—My mom hummed all the time, and I loved that she did. And being that I grew up with a hummer, I too was a hummer. "Was?" you may ask. And sadly "was" is the answer. You see, about nineteen or twenty years back, during the holiday season, two friends invited me to go to Barnes and Noble with them to shop. Back in the olden days, we had to go to actual, physical buildings that were bookstores in order to buy books—and I *loved* bookstores! Anyway, my two friends and I were wandering around in Barnes and Noble, and since I was in one of my favorite places to be, I was humming—Christmas carols to be specific. Well, these two friends were both sweet ladies who worried a lot about what other people thought, and one of them came up to me, tapped me on my shoulder, and said, "Do you realize you're humming out loud?" The way she said it made me feel terribly embarrassed and insecure—like I was being reprimanded by a librarian.

And from that day on, I never hummed in public again—*until* I began writing this book and thinking about my mom and how I loved that she hummed all the time. Mom always told me that humming and singing were signs of a happy heart. And although she also mentioned that unconscious humming could be a sign of mental illness (my mom was well read on any subject), she and I both understood that we hummed when our hearts were happy.

As you know, my mom passed away this past summer, after a long, long, long battle with dementia and Alzheimer's disease that was heartbreaking to watch her endure. I miss her every minute of every day. And yet there are times when I know she's with me, giving me strength and encouragement. And one day, very recently, during the writing of this book, I was at the store just browsing around for something, and I heard someone humming. Guess what? It was me! For whatever reason, there I was humming. And in that moment, my heart did feel happy. My happy heart had been scarred by my friend's pointing out to me that day that I was humming out loud (which translated to it was embarrassing her) and had made me so self-conscious. But I like to think that now I know my mom is out of pain, happy, and has her mind restored to her, there's a measure of happiness returned to my scarred-up little heart—a happiness that her example planted there. It's the only explanation I can come up with; though my heartache over losing my mom will never be completely healed, other heartaches have begun to heal now that she's all right again. I've caught myself humming other times here and there since then, and I hope someday I'll do it unconsciously the way I used to.

Snippet #3—Joe and Cynthia De Carlo owe their first names to (drumroll please) Kevin!!! Yep! I was naming the supporting characters in this book and found I was stuck on names for Keeley's parents. So I called out, "Kevin, what's the first man's name that comes to mind?" "Joe," he responded. "Okay…what's the first girl's name that comes to mind?" I asked. The first name he gave me was one I've already used. So I asked, "What's the second girl's name that comes to mind?" "Cynthia," he answered. Thus, Joe and Cynthia De Carlo were born!

Snippet #4—We actually have a bedroom that I call "The Cozy Cabin"! It has a sign above the door that says, "The Cozy Cabin," and although it's still a work in progress (it used to be the Star Wars room), it sure is cozy!

Snippet #5—When I was six years old, Johnny Depp wasn't famous yet, of course. However, I was head-over-heels in love with Jack Wild, a British actor famous for playing the Artful Dodger in the 1968 musical, *Oliver!* Of course, I was in love with him because of his staring role as Jimmy in the epic Sid and Marty Kroft creation, *H.R. Pufnstuf.* In fact I embarrassed my dad nearly to death when, at the age of six, I begged him to buy me a Tiger Beat teen magazine featuring Jack Wild on the cover at the grocery store. So, you see, I *totally* understand Paisley! She and I were six-year-old kindred spirits where romance is concerned!

Snippet #6—A couple of months ago, while I was going through a box of stuff I had packed away in 2005, I came across some old journal entries from the year I was eleven turning twelve. One of the entries I found really resonated with me, flashing back to the release of *Star Wars—A New Hope* in 1977. And although I loved this entry for so many reasons, what I didn't realize is how much my kids would enjoy it! In fact, my daughter laughed (out loud) several times every time she read it. However, because I didn't believe it was as funny as she thought it was, I posted the journal entry on my Facebook page. The result was a lot of comments telling me how funny it was; it also gave birth to the hashtag #BoomBoomFoxy. And so you see where Keeley and Paisley got boom-boom-foxy.

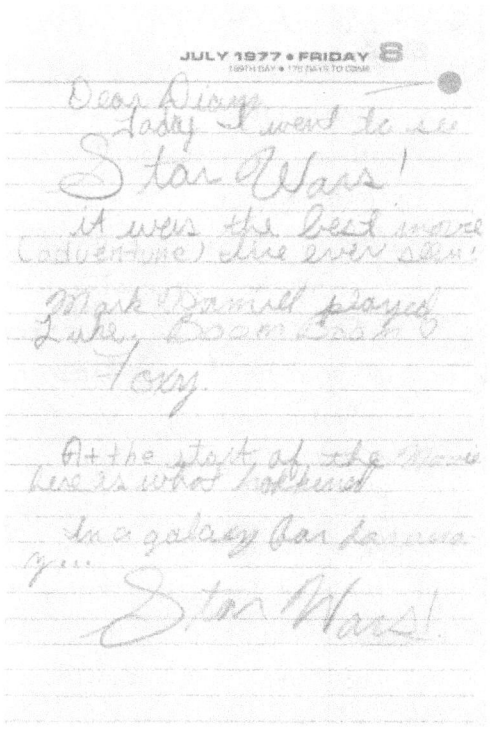

Snippet #7—I discovered an incredibly ambient, soothing, warm, wonderful "scent" while I was writing this book. While in Seattle visiting my close friend, we discovered a candle by Illume— Woodfire! Incredibly perfect for me! It smells exactly like a wood fire. Well, I lit it in my office and paired it with a Yankee Candle Jack Frost scent (peppermint and vanilla), and BAM! The perfect Winter Wonderland aroma! I burned through an entire Illume Woodfire candle. I just hope I can find more!

Snippet #8—Each and every one of Keeley's cousins on her father's side are named after pop music icons of the 1980s or Teen Scene actors of the 1990s. Debbie is named for Debbie Gibson, Tiffany is, of course, named after "Tiffany"—the one-named wonder who owned the mall scene in the late 1980s. Here enter the stars of *The Breakfast Club*, as Keeley's cousin Molly is my first nod to *The Breakfast Club* and '80s teen star Molly Ringwald. Anthony is the second TBC nod, to Anthony Michael Hall. Then we have the third TBC name, Judd for Judd Nelson. However, Judd's last name? You've got it! Sutherland, after Kiefer Sutherland. Then there's cousin Matthew, whose namesake Matthew Broderick played Ferris Bueller. Corey is my nod to Corey Feldman for the fact that I love *The Goonies* and *The 'Burbs* so much! Justine Bateman just popped up on Google when I searched for the top stars of the 1990s, and of course Ethan Hawke of *White Fang* fame popped up on that same list—thus, Ethan. And last, but certainly not least, is Ricky, named for Rick Schroder, who grew from being a cute little kid in the '80s to quite the handsome fellow as an adult. I know it's all nuts, but sometimes when I need a group of names for characters that really aren't going to be big players in a book, I draw from nostalgia! NOT a surprise to you, I'm sure.

Snippet #9—The name of Sutter's sleigh-pulling horse, Stackhouse, was inspired by two things. Thing one is that Stackhouse Orchards makes the delicious Raspberry Honey Almonds that I love so much and that inspired part of *Take a Walk with Me*. Thing two is that Stackhouse is one of the many nicknames that my sons have bestowed upon my husband.

Snippet #10—Just thought I'd offer a little "Jingle Bells" history/trivia for you! "Jingle Bells" was written in 1857 by James Lord Pierpont, specifically for Thanksgiving! It was originally titled "One Horse Open Sleigh" and was released in autumn of that year. It was first performed in Boston—on Washington Street—and it was decades before it became associated with the holiday season in general, especially Christmas. For quite a while it was often used as a drinking song—mostly at parties—and people would "jingle" their eyes around in their glasses as they sang it. Now the Medford Historical Society has long maintained that "Jingle Bells" was inspired by the town's very popular sleigh races of the nineteenth century.

VERSE 1:
Dashing through the snow
On a one horse open sleigh,
O'er the fields we go,
Laughing all the way.
Bells on bob tail ring,
making spirits bright.
O what sport to ride and sing
A sleighing song tonight.

CHORUS:
Oh, jingle bells, jingle bells,
Jingle all the way.
Oh, what joy it is to ride
In a one horse open sleigh.
Jingle bells, jingle bells,
Jingle all the way.
Oh, what fun it is to ride
In a one horse open sleigh.

VERSE 2:
A day or two ago
I tho't I'd take a ride,

And soon Miss Fannie Bright
Was seated by my side.
The horse was lean and lank.
Misfortune seemed his lot.
He got into a drifted bank
And we—we got upsot.

VERSE 3: (Often skipped verse is…)
The story I must tell
I went out on the snow,
And on my back I fell;
A gent was riding by
In a one-horse open sleigh.
He laughed as there I sprawling lie,
But quickly drove away.

VERSE 4:
Now the ground is white.
Go it while you're young,
Take the girls tonight,
and sing this sleighing song;
Just get a bobtailed bay,
Two forty as his speed,
Hitch him to an open sleigh,
And crack! You'll take the lead.

("Two forty" means that at trot, the horse would cover a mile in two minutes and forty seconds—i.e., 22.5 mph.)

P.S. In 1965, "Jingle Bells" was the very first song to be broadcast from space! Wally Schirra and Tom Stafford—the astronauts of Gemini 6—pranked Mission Control by sending this first:

Gemini VII, this is Gemini VI. We have an object, looks like a satellite going from north to south, up in a polar orbit. He's in a very low trajectory traveling from north to south and has a very high climbing ratio. It looks like it might even be a ... Very low. Looks like he might be going to reenter soon. Stand by one... You might just let me try to pick up that thing.

The two astronauts had a smuggled, teeny-weeny (or tiny weenie, as my grandsons say) harmonica (one inch long by three-eighths inch wide) and sleigh bells with them and proceeded to broadcast their own little version of "Jingle Bells." Fun, right?

Snippet #11—"Dipshidiot" is a term my friend and Party Posse member Stacey taught to me several years ago! The first time I heard her utter this slang term for someone who was being an idiot (or, as my dad would say, "a dip sh—"), I literally laughed out loud! It's so perfectly descriptive of some of those people we all stumble across in life, you know?

Snippet #12—There may in fact be a few raised eyebrows out there, being that I did finally allow one of my heroes to utter the word *shit*. However, before conniption fits run rampant, I will tell you a little story about how some things are one thing to one person and quite another to another person—even though both things are equal. So although I was born in Albuquerque, my parents and grandparents were all farmers, ranchers—you know, salt-of-the-earth, rural folks. I was a farm kid for a while as well, and actually, I'm still a farm kid at heart. Once a farm kid, always a farm kid. I think a lot of you will understand that. Anyway, as you know, my mom was a saint, an angel with nary a flaw—none that I ever saw—and anyone who knew her will tell you that. Why I mention my mom is for this reason: farmers cuss, ranchers cuss, horsemen cuss, cattlemen cuss. And yet I challenge anyone to find more God-fearing, hard-working, family-oriented people in all the world. Thus, when I was growing up (and I'll quote from one of my favorite books/movies), as Jean Shepherd said in *In God We Trust, All Others Pay Cash* (book)/*A Christmas Story* (movie based on the book), "In the heat of battle, my father wove a tapestry of obscenity that for all we know is still hanging in space over Lake Michigan." Yep! My dad was a cussing, swearing farmer/cattleman. My mom, on the other hand, was, as I said, an angel. Oh, she dropped an occasional Bible swear word, but not very often and never anything else. So the fact that I was raised to be aware that there were two f-words, not just one, comes into play here. My mother and father would've dropped dead if I had ever uttered either of the f-words: the "f---" word or the "fart" word. Either one would caused a fit of apoplexy in my family. However, once Kevin and I were married, and even though he was never allowed to say either f-word growing up either, the second f-word (fart—it still stings my ears to this day) had become so commonplace in society that Kevin saw no problems with it. But if I happened to drop a hammer on my toe and string out a "ssshhhiiii—," you would've thought I'd shot him. Oh, the lectures I got in those early years of marriage about the sh-- word—too many to enumerate, I'll guarantee that. Until one day, I said to my lovie-dovie, hunk-of-burnin'-love husband, "I'll tell you what, Kevin. When you quit saying *fart*, I'll quit saying *shit*." To which Kevin retaliated, "They are not the same! They are nothing alike! *Shit* is a bad word!" To which I countered, "They are both a slang term for a bodily function. So

152

there really is no difference." At this point in the conversation—crickets. More crickets. Now, do *not* take this to mean that I condone profanity—I do not. And our world had become so wrought with it that it is rotting. Still, to me a well-placed d-word, h-word, or s-word is less sinful than sitting in self-righteous judgment over someone else. My parents and grandparents were the best sort of people—far more obedient and striving for righteousness than most people I know. Therefore, my allowing Sutter to be himself and utter one cuss word when Judd was being a dipshidiot is my small tribute to those who went before me—those who taught me, guided me, and most importantly loved me unconditionally and forever! Here's to you, Dad—and Mom won't mind a bit!

Snippet #13—Just curious as to whether anyone realized from where I gleaned Sutter's cell phone number. The area code, 208, really is the Idaho area code. However, did anyone notice that the rest of his number, 867-5309, is *very* familiar? Ha ha! I love the '80s!

Snippet #14—Sutter and Keeley's owling excursion is my nod to Jane Yolen's beautifully written book *Owl Moon*. It's a lovely, lovely book that I adore!

Snippet #15—The discussion that Sutter and Keeley have concerning the song "Baby, It's Cold Outside" comes directly from my own irritation with the world polluting good things, as well as my research. Rest assured, that song was not written as a date rape song, a sexual assault song, or anything other than flirtation and a desire for men and the women to spend more time together. If you've never watched the old MGM musical *Neptune's Daughter*, you should! It's so fun!

Snippet #16—The Legos therapy that Sutter's mom comes up with to help with his mild PTSD is based on an actual experience one of my own kids had. I won't go into detail because it's a personal story for us. Just trust me—building Legos can help a person sort out a lot of things. There's so much time to think but also time not to think, to just concentrate on building and give your life worries a rest. In line with that, Keeley and Sutter's experiences with the Myers-Briggs Couples Personality Type tests and books is also based on my real-life, and I might add very liberating, experience with Myers-Briggs. I am an INFP, and Kevin is and ISFJ. Just a little personality trivia for you.

Snippet #17—I have a friend who went on a date on New Year's Eve with a guy she'd never been out with before. It was also a blind date set up for them by a mutual friend. By the next morning—New Year's Day—they were engaged! To my count, I believe they've been married over thirty years. As I often tell you, truth really is more astonishing than fiction sometimes.

Snippet #18—In 1992 my daughter was five years old and in kindergarten. She had the most wonderful kindergarten teacher in the world, and I felt extra blessed when my oldest son was privileged to have that same teacher a few years later. And although that special teacher touched our lives forever, and very profoundly in many ways, one of our favorite things she gifted us was a *phantasmagorical* recipe for poppy seed bread. It is *delicious*! It works perfectly as muffins too, and I think the thing that makes it so special is the orange glaze. Knowing how everyone loves yummy stuff, I've included the recipe here. Thank you so much, Darci White—for giving us a family tradition that has stuck for over twenty-five years!

Darci White's Poppy Seed Bread/Muffins

Ingredients:
3 cups flour
1 ¼ cups sugar
3 eggs
1 ½ cup milk
1 ⅛ cups oil
1 ½ teaspoons salt
1 ½ teaspoons baking powder
1–2 tablespoons poppy seeds
1 ½ teaspoons vanilla extract
1 ½ teaspoons almond extract

Mix ingredients. Bake in muffin cups 15 to 18 minutes at 350–400°F, or bake in loaf pans at 350°F (two large for 1 hour and 10 minutes or four small for 45 minutes). Let cool for 10 minutes, and then drizzle Orange Glaze (below) over tops. Let glaze soak into bread before removing from pans.

Ingredients for Glaze:
¼ cup orange juice
½ cup sugar
½ teaspoon vanilla extract
½ teaspoon almond extract

To my hero and inspiration…
Kevin from Heaven!

ABOUT THE AUTHOR

Marcia Lynn McClure's intoxicating succession of novels, novellas, and e-books—including *Shackles of Honor*, *The Windswept Flame*, *A Crimson Frost*, and *The Bewitching of Amoretta Ipswich*—has established her as one of the most favored and engaging authors of true romance. Her unprecedented forte in weaving captivating stories of western, medieval, regency, and contemporary amour void of brusque intimacy has earned her the title "The Queen of Kissing."

Marcia, who was born in Albuquerque, New Mexico, has spent her life intrigued with people, history, love, and romance. A wife, mother, grandmother, family historian, poet, and author, Marcia Lynn McClure spins her tales of splendor for the sake of offering respite through the beauty, mirth, and delight of a worthwhile and wonderful story.

BIBLIOGRAPHY

A Bargained-For Bride

Beneath the Honeysuckle Vine

A Better Reason to Fall in Love

The Bewitching of Amoretta Ipswich

Born for Thorton's Sake

The Chimney Sweep Charm

A Cowboy for Christmas

A Crimson Frost

Daydreams

Desert Fire

Divine Deception

Dusty Britches

The Fragrance of Her Name

The General's Ambition

A Good-Lookin' Man

The Haunting of Autumn Lake

The Heavenly Surrender

The Highwayman of Tanglewood

Indebted Deliverance

Kiss in the Dark

Kissing Cousins

The Light of the Lovers' Moon

Love Me

The Man of Her Dreams

Midnight Masquerade

The Object of His Affection

An Old-Fashioned Romance

One Classic Latin Lover, Please

The Pirate Ruse

The Prairie Prince

The Rogue Knight

Romance at the Christmas Tree Lot

Romance in a Winter Wonderland

Romance in Sleepy Hollow

The Romancing of Evangeline Ipswich

Romance with a Side of Green Chile

Romance with the Summer Son

Saphyre Snow

The Secret Bliss of Calliope Ipswich

Shackles of Honor

The Stone-Cold Heart of Valentine Briscoe

Sudden Storms

Sweet Cherry Ray

Take a Walk with Me

The Tide of the Mermaid Tears

The Time of Aspen Falls

To Echo the Past

The Touch of Sage

The Trove of the Passion Room

The Unobtainable One

Untethered

The Visions of Ransom Lake

Weathered Too Young

The Whispered Kiss

With a Dreamboat in a Hammock

The Windswept Flame

The Wolf King